One

Jill Barton was oblivious to the loud knocks and the hysterical shouts of her bridesmaids. She had to use all her concentration to keep her own hysteria under control. Jilted! She had been left waiting at the altar! What a fool she had been, standing there like some ninny, waiting. It was the pity in the minister's eyes that finally told her what she had been dreading. Deke wasn't going to show up. It was hard to be believed — Deke had been so insistent, so certain, telling her she needed a man in her life — that *he* was that man. She could almost hear his voice, so close to her ear: "You need me, Jill. The business world is no place for a girl like you. We can make it together. I know we can. I've wanted to ask you long before this, but there were always financial considerations. Now, with that little inheritance of yours, those problems are solved. Trust me, Jill, bells aren't supposed to go off in your head when I kiss you. That kind of love comes later, after marriage." His persuasive voice had whispered those words, banishing her doubts, gratifying her inner longings for marriage and family. "All your friends are married," Deke had continued, his lips nuzzling her ear. It was true, when they went to visit friends she was uncomfortable, feeling left out, as though she were missing something or someone. It was the intimacy, the sharing, that she wanted. Quietly, with a kiss, she had agreed to become Deke's wife.

Twenty-three was *time* to get married. It was *time* to start a family and put down roots. This, she thought, looking around the tiny apartment, was hardly what a person could call roots. Her job, while assured for the moment, could never be labeled as security. Each day she went to work she didn't know if her temperamental boss would fire her or not. If her copy was good, he would smile; but if it wasn't up to par, he would say there were thousands, yes, thousands of people who would jump at the chance to work for the Vancouver Advertising Agency. It was true. And they could all have the job if they wanted it. She didn't like the job, didn't want the pressure. Marriage would have been a graceful escape from it all. *Would have been.*

"Jill, open the door! Please! We can't leave you like this. Come on now, open the door!" It was Nancy Evans, her maid of honor.

Paint Me Rainbows

Jill walked on leaden legs over to the door. She opened it a crack and spoke softly. "Go home, Nancy. I just want to be alone. I'm all right. I plan to have a really good screaming and yelling tantrum where I cry and throw things. I might even roll around on the floor. After that I'll be all right. Don't worry about me. Tell Sue and Mary to take all the food home with them and thank them for being so understanding."

"I will, Jill. You're sure, now, that you'll be all right?"

"No, I'm not sure if I'll be all right. I'm going to try." Her voice cracked and then became firm. "I might just take off for somewhere. I'll send you a card or call you. Please, I want all of you to leave now." There was desperation in her voice. What would she do now? She had already left her job and had been disgraced in front of her friends.

"Okay, Jill. If there's anything I or the girls can do, just call us. Promise me and then I'll leave."

"I promise, Nancy." Tears were burning her eyes again. Leave, her mind shrieked. Leave so I don't have to hear the pity in your voice.

Jill gasped when she heard the filtered words through the door. "I knew it was too good to be true. You owe me five dollars,

Sue. I bet you that Deke wouldn't go through with the wedding, and I was right. What a rotten thing for him to do. The least he could have done was call Jill and tell her the wedding was off and not put her through this humiliation."

"You're right, Nancy. I don't know why I even bothered to make the wager. Everyone in the office was so sure this wedding would never come off. Jill was the only one who didn't seem to have even one small doubt. I feel so sorry for her. I just wish there was something we could do, but I know that Jill needs to be alone now to sort out her emotions."

"Forget the five dollars. I'm just sorry that I ever made that silly bet in the first place. It was a terrible thing for us to do. Jill is our friend. What we should have done was tell her what a bounder Deke really is. That would have been a real favor for our friend."

"I didn't have the nerve, Nancy," Sue all but squealed. "Besides, there was always the hope that Deke was serious about the wedding and truly did love Jill. Whatever, it's over and done with now. The best thing we can do is leave Jill as she suggested. In her own way she'll cope with all of this. If she needs us for anything, she knows where we are."

Jill closed her eyes. They all knew. Even the people in the office. How they must have watched the wedding preparations proceed and even counted down the days. Would he or wouldn't he go through with the wedding? How degrading, how humiliating.

A long sigh escaped her as she waited for the sound of the apartment door to close. They meant well, but the look in the minister's eyes was all the pity she could handle for one day. Her eyes fell to the stack of luggage next to the door. She was packed. All she had to do was walk out the door behind the girls. Everything had been taken care of. The elderly lady down the hall had promised to come in every day to feed her tropical fish and water the plants. The post office was going to hold her mail. Even the newspaper and milk deliveries had been canceled.

The loud sound of the front door closing made Jill's shoulders slump. They were gone and she was truly alone. Alone to take out her hurt and humiliation in the small apartment. What was it she had told Nancy? That she was going to throw a tantrum and kick and scream. Why? What was the point? It was over, finished. Why make herself more miserable, more angry? She had to start new, get on with her life! If she didn't do it now, this minute, she would stay locked up in this apartment that was full of Deke and memories of him. Before she could change her mind, she opened the bedroom door and then picked up the two suitcases.

The tweed luggage, her gift to herself, rested in the back of her yellow compact car. Her pocketbook was in the bucket seat on the passenger side. She took another deep breath, turned the key and maneuvered the small car from the curb. She would drive until she was exhausted and then stop.

Deftly, without a wasted motion, she slipped a cassette into the tape deck. Strains of romantic music rose and soared within the confines of the small car. Hastily, Jill withdrew the cassette and replaced it with her new disco tape. That was better.

She drove steadily north, her mind blank as she kept her eyes on the road and the beautiful autumn colors.

It was three hours later when her neck began to ache that she realized for the first time that she was still wearing her wedding gown and veil. A rich bubble of laughter escaped her. Some new life she was starting. Dumb. It was a dumb thing to do. No wonder people had smiled at her whenever she slowed down for traffic. She would have to risk the amused glances of gas station attendants when she stopped for gas.

She drove for another hour before she saw what she considered to be a suitable gas station. "Fill it up, and please let me have the key to the ladies' room," Jill said in a firm voice that brooked no questions. She slid from behind the wheel and gathered up her long train. Regally, she tripped her way to the washroom, only to remember halfway there that she needed her suitcase. A grimace on her face, she made her way back to the car and grabbed for the smaller of the two cases. "Please check the oil too." Not for the world would she let her eyes meet those of the attendant. What must he be thinking? Someday when I'm old and gray I'm going to write the memoirs of Jill Barton, she muttered as she fit the key into the bathroom door. The room was clean but cramped. Impatiently, she struggled and tugged at the heavy satin. Free of its stranglehold, she felt a hundred percent better. She balanced the suitcase on the sink and manipulated the numbers of the combination lock to her birthdate. Just the sight of her jeans and the pullover shirt made her feel better. This was her style. A pair of sneakers for added comfort was all she needed. Now, what was she to do with the gown and gossamer veil?

There was no way she could fit them into her suitcase, and she just couldn't leave them in a gas station washroom. She would throw them in the back seat for the time being. Perhaps the day would come when she could put all of this behind her and have a use for them again. Her back straightened and her eyes spewed sparks. It would be a very long time indeed. She had made a fool of herself. Once was enough. There wouldn't be a second time.

The heavy gown and veil were on her arm, the suitcase in her other hand, as she made her way back to the car. She offered no explanation to the curious attendant as she paid for her gas and a quart of oil.

Back on the highway she realized she was getting hungry. She didn't want to stop, because that would mean talking to people and she wanted only to be alone with her thoughts. She wanted to be insulated from everything and anything. The car was working its own brand of quiet magic as it ate up the miles on the highway.

She drove for another two hours and then pulled over to the side of the road. She would just take a little catnap. She couldn't keep her eyes open another minute.

It was still dark when she woke. The digital watch glowed with red numerals. It was

3:30 — the middle of the night. After rubbing the sleep from her eyes with one hand while she turned on the ignition and lights, she continued to drive steadily north with no destination in mind.

Dawn broke softly, casting streams of reddened sunlight across the dew-drenched countryside. Jill Barton yawned sleepily, tightening her hold on the steering wheel of her mud-splattered car. Squinting her eyes, she forced herself to concentrate on the stretch of road in front of her. She had been driving aimlessly for hours and realized suddenly that she hadn't passed another car for miles. Instead of feeling threatened by the thought of having the road to herself, she was buoyed by a thrilling surge of freedom. Even a flat tire at this point wouldn't dampen her spirits. Jill smiled as she thought about the prospect of such a mishap. She was totally prepared for any mechanical disaster her car might decide to present her with. Night classes at the community college had made her an expert on the basics of servicing motor vehicles. She could change a tire faster than a twenty-year man at a mechanic's shop. Her knowledge of all the intricacies of just what made her car purr along so happily was so impressive that even Deke had had to admit that she was a born grease monkey.

Now that she had been jilted — must have something to do with her name — and had burned her bridges behind her, it was time to look her situation full in the face. And it was time to take a look at Deke and what had happened to her yesterday.

Deke had never been perfect, far from it. He was bound to be a success, there was no point in denying it; his drive had earned him a secure position in the advertising business. Deke had started low in the ranks only five years previously and used his wit and charm to his own advantage. Jill had been enticed by him from the start. His personality was almost overwhelming. Assured and confident, he seemed to lack any faults or idiosyncrasies. His face was actually quite unremarkable, but his blue eyes gleamed with a boyish mischievousness, making him the prime target for all the single girls in the office. Some of the girls were so blatant in their approaches to him that Jill had learned with a jolt that she wasn't the only one who harbored coffee-break fantasies about him.

Of course, Jill held no secret hopes of being singled out by him. It wasn't that she didn't consider herself worthy of his attentions; she knew that she had the type of looks that turned men's heads. Her hair cascaded down her back in silken blond strands. The practice of confining the length in plaits before bed each night gave the tresses a beautiful series of waves, causing some of her friends to refer to her teasingly as Rapunzel. Her eyes were a muted green, sparking into flashing embers when someone tried her temper. In an age of elaborate makeup and chic hairstyles, Jill felt content to pat a smidgen of face powder across her countenance and dab just her lips with color. In many respects Jill was a woman who combined a little of the good old-fashioned ways with an ample helping of liberated ideas. She enjoyed her independence, yet knew that she craved a real family life. At times she chided herself for her thoughts of puttering around a kitchen stocked with an array of copper pots, potted herbs and bubbling concoctions from exotic cookbooks. She could almost picture herself in a red gingham apron, greeting that special someone at the door with a long, romantic kiss. But just as quickly as it would seize her, the vision would shimmer and fade.

There was another side of Jill that seemed in complete contradiction to the rest of her. Some people called it impulsiveness, but Jill knew that she had been blessed with an adventurous spirit. Whenever things caught her fancy, she pursued them. On a dare once she had joined a friend in a sky-diving course, ending up promising herself that learning to fly would be next on her agenda. She followed whims with a passion, never passing up a chance to learn something new.

Jilted! Left waiting at the altar! That was new, wasn't it? How humiliating. If she had to blame something for Deke's desertion of her at the critical hour, it was probably her impulsiveness. He wanted a doormat, someone who would yes him to death and never have a thought of her own. Even her ten thousand dollars wasn't enough to make him want her on a forever basis.

In all honesty, Jill knew in her heart of hearts that she had been less than wholeheartedly enthusiastic about the wedding. Things had moved so fast that she hadn't taken time to examine her inner true feelings.

She should have run like a deer the day the office started to buzz about a new advertising account that all the head executives were hoping to land. The competition had been fierce, the reward a hefty commission and a step up the corporate ladder. When word had reached the floor that Deke had pulled off the biggest coup of his career, the oohs and aahs had seemed almost perfunctory. Jill had remembered thinking that it would only be a matter of time before this advertising whiz had reins on the entire company. For some reason she felt a surge of anger take hold of her when he had paused beside her desk that night as she was covering her typewriter and sorting out her work for the next morning. She had looked up at him, trying to feign boredom as she waited for him to speak. No doubt he wanted some last-minute typing done for his new account, and Jill was silently coaching herself to be assertive and refuse him outright. Instead, he had laughed, almost nervously, a lock of his hair falling out of place and across his eyes.

"Ummm, yes . . . Miss Barton," he had said haltingly, "I suppose you've heard about my landing the Becker account."

"Yes, Mr. Atkins," Jill had answered dutifully. "Congratulations."

"What I'm trying to say, Miss Barton . . . Jill, isn't it? I'd like to ask you to help me celebrate this evening."

"Mr. Atkins," Jill whispered. "You don't even know me except in passing. . . ."

"Before you turn me down flat, let me explain." His eyes dancing with a contagious enthusiasm, Deke had begun to shift his weight from one foot to the other, reminding Jill of a teenager eager to learn a new dance step. "I'm so elated about landing that account that I can't waste it just on me. So I told myself, 'Go out and find the prettiest girl you can and take her out on the town.' So, of course, I thought of you immediately. What do you say? Make it your good deed for the day. I promise you, it'll be a night you won't forget. We'll hit all the high spots. An elegant dinner, dancing, the whole schmeer!"

Feeling a smile tug at the corner of her lips, Jill had relented. "All right, Mr. Atkins, your talents as a salesman do seem to be above par."

"You'll accept, then?" Deke had grinned.

"Chalk it up to your winning ways," she had answered teasingly.

When word had filtered down that Deke had lost the account, Jill had found herself in complete sympathy with him. She had pampered him, coddled him, told him over and over that it was a minor setback and he would learn from his mistake. Long walks, with her doing all the talking to rebuild his confidence and catering to his every wish and whim so he wouldn't dwell on what he called his "personal rejection" by his superiors, seemed to be all she had had time for for weeks on end.

As far as the office was concerned, Jill and Deke had become a definite item.

She had found herself becoming more and more involved in his life, yet somehow she had been nagged with the feeling that the Deke she was seeing was only part of the man. Quick glimpses of him when he had had all his barriers down had made Jill wonder if there were facets to his personality that he struggled desperately to keep in check. His impatience with Jill's involvement in night classes at the university and club meetings that took her away from the apartment had been one cause of many a ruined evening and countless bruised feelings. Deke had referred to her interests as flights of whimsy, seeming not to realize or care how much his judgments wounded her. A part of her had felt love for Deke, and another had felt resentment and annoyance that he didn't even bother to try to understand her and her needs. While he had acted oblivious to her inner turmoil, his concern had centered on company obligations. Jill had been convinced that he loved her; after all, he had said it so easily. He had found time for her and had told her that she made everything in his life seem worthwhile and enjoyable. That was what convinced her in the end.

And then had come the big day and the big check. How readily she had fallen in with his plans. She hadn't balked when he had suggested Hawaii for a honeymoon. What was three thousand dollars when she was starting off on a whole brand new life? And she did love him, didn't she? She always had a queasy feeling in her stomach when Deke was due for a date, and her heart pounded when he called her on the phone. And the final argument in favor of love was that her eyes had misted each and every time he had whispered, "I love you."

This recollection, this journey to what might have been, was something she had to put behind her. From now on, each day would be regarded as the first day of the rest of her life.

The tape deck kept her company for the next several hours as she guided the smoothly running car farther north. If she stopped for lunch and spent half an hour eating, she would still make the border of Rhode Island by midafternoon. She hummed her approval along with the music.

The rich golds and browns of the autumn leaves were having a hypnotic effect on Jill. She felt peaceful, almost content, as the minutes sped by. It was a miracle that she wasn't weeping and wailing, and near to total collapse, at what had happened to her yesterday.

Jill drove on, hour after hour, stopping at midafternoon on a wide shoulder of the road. Her intention was to close her eyes for only a few seconds to ward off the bright afternoon autumn glare.

Two

The crunch of gravel beneath the car wheels stirred Jill from her restless slumber. Raising her head to peer out at the source of the commotion, she grinned sheepishly at an elderly woman tapping on the windshield.

Rolling down her window just far enough to enable her to hear the woman speak, Jill said groggily, "What is it?"

The old woman squinted her eyes, a gnarled finger coming up to her nose in an unconscious gesture as she pushed her bifocals up and leaned down for a closer inspection of Jill. "My lord, honey!" she squawked. "I thought you were dead . . . looked it from the way you were slumped over that steering wheel. Can't tell these days, you know. Seems like girls your age are always barking up the wrong tree and getting themselves in trouble. You're taking your life in your hands sleeping in your car like that, dearie."

Jill felt a scalding blush start at her neck and flow upward. Imagine being scolded by a complete stranger!

"You mark my words, young lady," the woman continued as she marched back to her own car, "you'd best be more careful next time. In my day you had to worry about being carted off by gypsies. Goodness knows what fates you're tempting nowadays!"

It took Jill a good ten minutes to recover from the woman's well-meaning tirade, and as she straightened her hair as best she could without digging in her tote bag for her hairbrush she promised herself that her immediate goal was to find a place to stay for the coming night.

Pulling back onto the road, Jill glanced at her surroundings. The road snaked out in tight curves, hinting that her hasty retreat from southern New Jersey the day before hadn't brought her too far. A mist shrouded the countryside, making the smell of dampened earth permeate the inside of the car. Jill always drove with the window down, even in the most inclement weather. Traffic began to pick up, and she glanced toward her gas gauge. She was down to a quarter of a tank, which didn't mean much since her car had never registered correctly. For all she knew she could be close to running on empty. Coasting around a bend in the road, Jill smiled as she saw signs of a town up ahead, recognition lighting the pupils of her eyes as the next sign she passed stated simply, Mill Valley. A small, picturesque village community, Mill Valley had become a popular retreat for artistic people of all sorts, or so the roadside plaque proclaimed.

It didn't take long for Jill's unease to melt into enchantment as she guided her car along the narrow streets of Mill Valley. Passing several establishments she knew she had to inspect more carefully, she spied a tight parking place along the main boulevard and eased her car into it with enviable expertise. Her first adventure came in the guise of a combination curio shop and clothing store. Making a point to ferret out the predictable rack of postcards by the cash register, Jill picked out several at random, garnering local information from them. Knowing that the wardrobe she had packed was mostly resort wear, Jill purchased two hand-embroidered sweater tops and a rather unique denim skirt that had been fashioned out of a pair of old jeans and extended with a floral print material. Tourist prices had taken their toll, and Jill held back a gasp as the girl behind the checkout counter let a hefty sum roll off her tongue to punctuate the clanging jangle of the old-fashioned cash register. Watching the girl methodically fold her purchases and slip them into a paper bag, Jill couldn't help but feel that for the price she was paying the goods should be packed in velvet and delivered to her door with a complimentary bottle of champagne.

As she clutched the bag to her side, Jill's rumbling stomach reminded her that lunch the previous day had been her last acquaintance with food. Directly across the street was a health-food store that from all appearances seemed to be doing quite a brisk business. Dodging traffic, Jill eyed the outside of the shop. The windows were filled with all kinds of greenery and rough-hewn log siding gave it a quaint look of being from another time. A swinging sign hung over the opened doorway, and Jill could imagine the sound its metal hinges would make in a stiff wind. Nature's Bounty was the name the proprietor had chosen for the establishment, and as Jill stepped inside she found herself agreeing with the christening. Barrels overflowed with offerings of all kinds. Herbs grew happily in hundreds of little pots, waiting to be clipped for use, and a large refrigerated bin lined the back of one wall, laden with yogurts, natural juices and milk products. Jill decided to introduce her taste buds to some new fare, so on an impulse she selected an avocado sandwich on whole wheat bread and a small carton of a strawberry health drink made with yogurt. She had always preferred yogurt over ice cream, feeling righteous when she satisfied her cravings with fresh fruit stirred into the plain variety instead of weakening to a hot fudge sundae with nuts. Accepting the offer of a straw as she paid for her late lunch, Jill opened the drink and took a preliminary sip. It tasted good, tart and sweet at the same time.

Tucking her sandwich into her tote bag to be sampled when she had settled back into her car, Jill hung her bag on one shoulder and wedged her package under the same arm so she could sip her drink more easily. Closing her eyes as she savored the next swallow, Jill stood poised in the doorway to the shop. A gruff jostling was her first indication that she was blocking the entrance. Before she could react, she had been roughly pushed aside, some of the drink splashing against her shirt.

The culprit who had so rudely broken her trance walked with long strides up to the counter, his presence demanding immediate attention. Jill stared at the man's back, willing him to turn around to acknowledge what he had done so she could have the satisfaction of demanding an apology. As though sensing the intensity of her thoughts, the man turned, fixing Jill with a cold, penetrating gaze that made her words catch in her throat. He was undoubtedly the most attractive man she had ever seen. His hair was dark, the color of a moonless night. His eyes smoldered black, sparking a luminous shade as he let them travel the length of her, coming to rest even with her eyes in a penetrating challenge.

"You could have at least said excuse me!" Jill stated with more conviction than she felt.

The man seemed to consider her for a moment longer, a mocking grin curling along his lips. "On the contrary, miss," he cooed in a flagrant tease, "you were the one blocking the doorway." Without another word he turned back to the counter, having issued what he considered to be an appropriate dismissal.

Jill knew the urge to throw something — anything — just as long as she could make it hit its mark. Deciding reluctantly against violence, her quick mind devised another plan. Walking slowly to where the man stood, Jill paused for a brief second before she slowly and deliberately poured the remaining contents of the carton over his shoes, creating little puddles of cream where he stood. Not waiting for his reaction, she turned and left the shop, jogging out to her car.

"Men!" she mumbled as she struggled with the key, finally turning over the ignition with more power than necessary. "The arrogance . . . just because they're born male they think all women are put on earth to suit their whims."

Trying to squelch the anxiety that the incident had spurred in her, Jill occupied her mind with thoughts of a place to stay. There were countless accommodations in town, but none seemed to suit her basic prerequisites. First of all, it had to be cheap. She had to be frugal now since she had made the decision not to go back to the office. But more important than anything else, it had to be far enough away from the mainstream. Whenever she needed to think things out, she found that long, lonely walks helped. Jill knew that there must be a beach within close distance of Mill Valley, so she turned her car in that direction.

Certain that her search was going to prove totally futile, Jill had almost resolved herself to turning back to Mill Valley and settling for one of their tourist-class motels when a stark black and white sign along the side of the road caught her eye. The lettering on it was sharp and clear: Woodmeire Cottages. There was no telling how old the sign was, but Jill decided to follow the road until it ended. She had traveled more than a mile up the graveled road when she saw a cluster of buildings ahead, one boasting a clothesline that danced merrily with an array of shirts and pants.

Even before the car had sputtered to a stop, the door to what appeared to be the office opened and a squat little woman waddled out of the doorway and onto the porch.

"Get yourself lost?" she inquired happily as Jill stepped from the car.

Jill shook her head, knowing immediately that she liked the woman. "Actually, I was hoping to rent one of your cottages for a few weeks."

The old woman stared at Jill and at her long golden hair. She grimaced slightly. "It don't exactly work that way, Miss . . . what did you say your name was?"

"Jill Barton. I don't understand. You must have —" Jill looked around "— about twenty cottages here. Are they all full?"

"Lan'sakes, no, child. You must be from out of state, otherwise you would know what this place is." Her eyes twinkled as she watched a play of emotion on Jill's face.

"You mean . . . this quiet, beautiful place is . . . ?" Disbelief glowed on Jill's face. "I didn't know. What I mean is, there isn't any kind of sign to indicate . . ." she finished lamely.

The old woman laughed, this time doubling over. "This place has been referred to as many things, but I don't think it's ever been called what you're thinking. You was kind of thinking this was a nudist colony. Is that it?"

"You mean it isn't?" Jill answered the question with a question.

"Lordy, no. This is an *artists' colony.* I should have told you straight off. Living here for sixty-odd years makes me forget that everybody in the world don't know about it. By the way, my name is Agnes Beaumont. Everyone hereabouts calls me Aggie. I'm the housekeeper for the main house. See, that's the main house over there," she said, pointing to a white clapboard house nestled between evergreens. "I'm just sitting here in this little office to answer the phone till Mr. Matthews gets back. He went into town for some supplies and should be back any minute. He's the one you gotta talk to about staying here. You one of those artist types? What's your specialty?"

"My specialty?" Jill asked in amazement.

She still hadn't gotten over the shock that the place wasn't an out-and-out bordello.

"What do you do? Do you write or do you paint? We've got a sculptor here all the way from Los Angeles."

Jill's mind raced. "Write. Right, that's what I do. I write." She decided she could be comfortable with the small white lie. In a way she did write at the office. There was no need to tell anyone that she was no longer employed. As long as she had the money to pay the rent, what difference did it make? It wasn't going to be one of those long-term visits. She was just going to stay long enough to get her head on straight and her act together before she moved on.

"I thought so. I can spot a writer a mile away," Aggie said knowledgeably. "You writers all seem to have a vague kind of look, like you're always thinking about something and just waiting for a pencil to scribble it down."

"You're so right," Jill agreed hastily. "I'm always thinking and I never seem to have a pencil." Frantically, she tried to bring her thoughts into focus. "Do you think I'll have any trouble getting one of the cottages?"

"Shucks no, child. Long as you're one of those artsy people, no offense, you won't have no problem. Look, would you mind doing me a favor of sorts?" Not waiting for Jill to reply, Aggie rushed on. "I got nine blueberry pies ready to go in the oven. Logan, he loves my berry pie, and I want them properly cooled before dinner. That stove over at the main cottage has a mind of its own, and I couldn't take the chance of the pies spilling over and then smoking up the kitchen. We don't have any fire department around here to rush out to put out a fire. You just sit there. There's coffee in the pot — see," Aggie said, pointing to an ancient enamel pot sitting on a hot plate. "You just put your feet up on the desk the way Logan does and wait for him. I'll be seeing you at the dinner table."

"At the dinner table?" Jill asked, puzzled.

"Yep. We all eat in the main dining hall. I do the cooking, and I'm a pretty darn good cook. I don't know what's going to happen at the end of the week. I got to go to Seattle to help my niece have her baby. Logan is just going to have to get another cook or something. You just sit there now and wait for Logan; he should be here any minute."

She was gone, the screen door banging against the doorframe. Jill frowned. How did you help someone have a baby? If there was a way, she was sure the gregarious Aggie would know of it.

Jill poured herself a cup of coffee. She stared at the thick syrupy mess, trying to decide if it was indeed coffee or some kind of new black syrup. Tentatively, she sipped at it and choked. It tasted like turpentine and tar. If Aggie made blueberry pie the way she made coffee, it was no wonder the cottages were mostly empty.

Thumbing through tattered, dog-eared magazines, Jill chose a vintage copy of *Psychology Today.* She did as Aggie instructed and placed her feet on the desk and started to read the magazine.

"Where's Aggie?" a cold, hard voice demanded.

Jill blinked, taking in the tall form standing in the doorway. Her spirits plummeted when she recognized the man from the health-food store. Of all the rotten, miserable luck!

"Aggie is baking pies," Jill answered defensively. Quickly, she removed her feet from the battered desk. "I would like to rent one of the cottages." Thank God, he didn't seem to recognize her as the person who had dumped the strawberry yogurt drink all over his shoes.

A fly buzzed impatiently, its blue-black wings circling Logan Matthews' legs. Impatiently, he brushed at it, his face full of annoyance. "Damn pests," he muttered angrily. His eyes narrowed slightly as he advanced farther into the room. When he was inches from her, recognition dawned on him. Again, he lashed out at the offending fly. "It's your fault that this fly is driving me crazy. Look for a flyswatter — there must be one around here somewhere." It was an order, a command.

"You . . . you deserved to have that drink dumped all over you. Manners and a little courtesy would have helped. You just . . . you knocked me out of the way. You did. I almost fell," Jill snapped.

"Women! You're all alike. You want to be liberated. You want all of these rights, and then you complain when you get them. If you had stayed in the kitchen where you belonged, this wouldn't be happening."

"In the kitchen!" Jill shrieked.

"Yes, the kitchen. That's where women belong. Besides, you were blocking the doorway, drinking that mess without regard to who was coming or going. I didn't knock you over, I brushed past you. End. Fini. I don't want to hear another word. Get the flyswatter!"

"Get it yourself," Jill snapped as she gathered up her tote bag. "Just tell me where I register."

"You don't understand. You only register if I say you register."

"What does that mean?"

"That means you can't stay here unless you're an artist. What do you do?"

"I write," Jill said loftily. "How much is it for a week?"

Logan Matthews determinedly swatted at the angrily buzzing fly. "Let me see your credentials," Matthews said arrogantly. It was clear he didn't believe her.

"I don't have any . . . any credentials. I'm just starting out, and so far I don't have anything published. I'm reliable; I won't break your furniture and I don't have wild parties."

"If you don't have credentials, you can't stay here. How do I know you aren't some sort of runaway housewife out for a lark? We get them all the time. Sooner or later a husband shows up, and then there's hell to pay. If you don't have something to verify who you are, you can't stay here."

"That's just great. It's a good thing James Michener or Norman Mailer didn't stop here. You would certainly have pie on your face. Just look how famous they are. What I'm saying is, how can I ever hope to get to be like them if you won't give me a chance? They had to start out somewhere. I need the peace and quiet of a place like this." Her tone was desperate as she pleaded with the arrogant man standing next to her.

"What is it you're writing? Show me something, a draft, an outline, that will verify the fact that you're serious about all of this."

Jill noticed that his eyes were lowered to her left hand, looking for some sign of a ring.

"I haven't even started, so how can I show you something? All the ideas are in my head. I can pay."

Logan Matthews snorted. "This place is free. We don't take money. All the guests take turns with the chores. We don't have any freeloaders here. Right now, since summer has ended, we've only three artists in residence, so there's plenty of room. But the rules are the same. Everyone has to pull his weight. Why don't you tell me what it is you're writing? Then I'll make a decision."

Jill's mind raced. "My memoirs," she said softly.

Logan Matthews threw back his head and howled with laughter. "Your memoirs? What makes you think anyone would be interested in *your* memoirs?"

Jill's dander was up. "It doesn't make any difference if anyone is interested or not.

That's what I'm doing. I have led a very . . . a . . . diff . . . what I mean is, it's been a challenging kind of life. I think that I'm more than qualified to write about myself." Jill couldn't believe she was saying these things, lying actually. But somehow it was urgent that he believe she was a writer because it had suddenly become important that she be allowed to stay here in the colony.

There was humor in Matthews' face. "I get it — one of those trashy exposé things. Somehow, you don't look the type."

"You have no right to type me in any way. All I want is a cottage so I can start on my . . . on my book. Either you're going to give it to me or you aren't. What is it?"

"And you're feisty too. What kind of typewriter do you have? Electric or portable? Some of the cottages have electricity and some don't."

"I don't . . . have a typewriter, that is. I told you, I'm just starting out and I plan to work in longhand till I get the hang of the whole thing. What's wrong with that?" she asked defensively.

Matthews grinned. "I can hardly wait to read this work of art when it's finished. I'm going against my better judgment, I want you to know that. But you can stay. If I find out that you're in some sort of trouble or one of those runaway wives, you'll leave so fast this place will go up in smoke. Do we understand each other?"

Jill let her breath out in little doses. "Perfectly."

"You can have Briar Cottage. It has electricity. Let me see," he said, thumbing through a ledger. "I'll have to assign you to some chores. You will do all your tasks at the assigned time. When you pursue your . . . literary career will, of course, be up to you. Is that agreeable?"

Jill nodded.

"Starting in the morning, you will have latrine duty. When Aggie leaves for Seattle, you will have kitchen duty. And two of the guests are men who like to eat."

"Now, just a minute," Jill sputtered angrily.

"Take it or leave it. By the way, what's your name?"

"What's latrine duty? Jill Barton."

"Bathrooms, Jill Barton."

"Are you saying that the cottages don't have private bathrooms?"

"Right. Everything here is a communal project. We have a dining room, a workroom where each guest is assigned his or her own space and, of course, the bathrooms.

Showers, one tub. Then, of course, there's this office, and we have a motor pool of sorts. The men handle the yard work. Do you have any questions?"

"And if I did, what good would it do me?" Jill muttered under her breath.

"We breakfast at seven, lunch at noon, and dinner is served at six on the dot. Punctuality is a virtue. Can you remember that during your stay?" There was a mocking light in the dark eyes as Logan Matthews waited to see what her reaction would be. "Do you want to stay or not?"

"Okay. Okay," Jill said through clenched teeth.

"By the way, about the bathrooms. Cleaning supplies are in a closet at the main house."

"I thought they would be. What time do I report tomorrow?"

"Sunup should do it. Of course, if you want to get a head start and clean the bathroom before you turn in for the night, that's up to you. All I'm telling you is I want a clean bathroom when I get up in the morning. I shower at five-thirty in the morning."

Jill's eyes widened. "No one gets up that early."

"I do. Now, sign the register and I'll show you to your cottage. By the way, it's fairly secluded, allows for privacy. It's clean and comfortable."

Jill's hands were shaking so badly that she could barely sign her name on the dotted line. What in the world had she gotten herself into? By the time Aggie left for Seattle she would be right on her trail. Kitchen duty! It was a wonder he didn't call it KP. Latrines and KP. He must have been in the military at some point. Just who was he anyway? She made a mental note to quiz Aggie the first chance she got.

"Come along, then, I'll show you to your cabin. Where did you park your car?" Logan said, snapping his ledger shut after he had carefully scrutinized her writing.

"My car is . . ." A vision of her bridal gown in the back seat forced her back a step. Wedding gowns would no doubt fit into the same category as runaway wives. "Why . . . ah, why don't we walk to the cottage? That way I can look around and come back later for my car. I think I would like to walk. In fact, I know I would like to walk. Let's walk," she babbled nervously.

Logan noticed her uneasiness. "You don't have some kind of problem you aren't telling me about, do you?"

Jill looked at his knitted brows and blanched. "Me? Problem? Certainly not.

My life is an open book. In fact, it's such an open book that's why I am so willing to write about it." She was babbling again.

Logan opened the screen door and a large Irish setter bounded into the room, heading straight for Jill. He skidded to a stop and then daintily placed both paws on her shoulder. He licked her face affectionately, his tail wagging furiously. "This is Doozey. He's always been fond of girls, but I have to admit I've never seen him quite so smitten. Usually, he has more manners. Down, Doozey."

Jill wiped her face with the sleeve of her shirt. She liked dogs, and Doozey seemed the perfect companion to take on the long walks she planned.

"Go pester Aggie," Logan said warmly to the dog.

Hrumph, Jill snorted inwardly. Guess you have to be a dog to get any kind of friendliness from this guy. How handsome he was when his chiseled features softened. She liked the warm tone in his voice when he spoke to Doozey. For a brief moment she compared him to Deke and wasn't surprised when Deke came up short. But then, next to a man this handsome, most men would come up short.

Jill's nerves were atwitter as she walked

alongside Logan, each intent on his own thoughts. He unlocked the door to Briar Cottage and stood back. Jill loved its rustic, cheap comfort. She would be more than comfortable here. "You were right, it's very clean. I'll be sure to keep it that way."

"The bathrooms are at the end of the compound. To the left of the office is the dining room. In one sense it's inconvenient for Aggie because she has to cart all the food to the dining area. She does all the cooking in my kitchen. If I have the time, I help her or some of the other men pitch in."

"Wouldn't it be more efficient if you had a complete kitchen over there to work in?" Jill asked hesitantly as she visualized herself lugging heavy pots of food across the compound.

"The plans are underway. Aggie's getting older and I can't have her working so hard. The work should be completed by the end of next summer. Until then, you're young, hale and hearty, so you should have no problems. Just think," he said coolly, "this experience might take up a whole chapter in your memoirs."

He was baiting her. There was little doubt in her mind that Logan Matthews didn't believe a word she had said about writing a book. She bristled slightly and then relaxed.

For now, she was safe. Hard work never killed anyone. She could and would survive. As soon as he left, she would set out on that promised walk. And before she returned she would stop and see Aggie. Aggie should be a wealth of information on Logan Matthews and this colony. First rule of a writer: Always know what you're writing about. Certainly, that rule could be applied to this situation.

"If I stretch it out, I might be able to make two chapters," Jill answered tartly. "By the way, are you the manager of this colony, or exactly what do you do here?"

"Is this for your book too?"

"One never knows," Jill quipped.

"Why don't we just say I'm a patron of the arts and let it go at that?"

"If that's what you want to say, it's okay with me. I myself don't exactly need a patron, not at this point anyway," Jill said hastily.

"Do I take that to mean you are financially and economically independent?" Logan queried.

"More or less," Jill hedged. This was no time for him to delve into her background. So far, she had lucked out with a minimum of background on herself. But she had to get that gown out of her car as quickly as she could before he saw it and made an issue out of it.

"I'll see you in the dining room. Six sharp. Aggie has a lot to do, so perhaps you could help her clean up after dinner."

"Is that a suggestion or an order?"

"Whatever you want. Just do it," Logan said coldly as he closed the door behind him. She heard the dog bark happily and watched as Logan picked up a stick to toss in the air. The setter bounded off happily while Logan strode across the compound with long, purposeful strides. Jill knew in her gut that everything Logan did he would do purposefully.

Thirty minutes later the yellow car was parked outside Briar Cottage. The mound of white satin and the lacy veil were in a heap on the floor of the tiny hall closet. She hadn't realized how tense she was until the closet door clicked shut.

She still had two hours till dinner. She could take a walk over to the main house and visit Aggie. She would even magnanimously offer to help her if the older woman looked as though she could use another pair of hands.

Three

Doozey trotted alongside Jill in companionable silence. Every so often he would woof at a stray squirrel or chipmunk but make no move to chase it away. She was following him, Jill realized as they came near the compound. A rich, tangy aroma tantalized her senses. It was a rich New England kind of smell and one with which she was vaguely familiar. What was Aggie cooking? Evidently, Doozey was as curious as she was. He broke into a run and headed for the back of the Cape Cod house — toward the kitchen area, Jill surmised. She followed the dog and wasn't surprised to see Doozey in his begging position near the screen door.

"Hi, Aggie, it's me, Jill. Mr. Matthews said I could stay. I'm in Briar Cottage. May I come in?"

"Of course. My kitchen is open to anyone and everyone. Here, have a peanut butter cookie. Made them fresh this morning. Give one to that fool dog before his tongue falls out. He's just like Logan, can't keep either one of them away from my cookies. If I didn't keep an eye on this cookie jar, them two would eat them all before the day was out. Logan likes to take them with him in his knapsack when he goes off to do his thing."

"What smells so good, Aggie?"

"New England clam chowder, Aggie Beaumont style. What that means, child, is I put strips of bacon and a dash of celery seed in it. That makes it authentically mine. Everyone around here just calls it Aggie's chowder. Even that hound sitting next to you likes it. Where did you come across him?"

"Actually, he found me while I was walking and he sort of led me here. I would have sought you out myself; he just made it easier for me."

"So, you're in Briar Cottage. Been a long time since anyone's been in that place. Clean as a whistle, let me tell you." Aggie frowned. "I can't believe that he let you stay there. There are some cottages that aren't so far away."

"Is there something wrong with Briar Cottage?" Jill asked fearfully.

"Heavens no, child. It's just that Logan's fianceé lived there last summer. When she up and left, he closed it, and no one has been near it since."

"Mr. Matthews isn't married, then?"

"Nope, single and free as the breeze. Isn't that what you young people say? He's all caught up in his work. He's a very busy man. Runs a mighty big law firm in Boston when the spirit moves him. Come summer, he comes here and runs this place. He's rich as Rockefeller; that's why he lets everyone stay here for free as long as they pull their weight. He's a painter himself. Mighty fine artist. Does seascapes and trees. He paints a tree like an angel."

"Really? He didn't look like a painter to me."

"He's one of the best — right up there with Andrew Wyeth. Things here can tend to themselves. Come along to my room and I'll show you a picture he did just for me. His daddy and my husband used to run this place, and then when Logan came of age he sort of took over, him being a painter and all."

Jill followed Aggie down a hall and then down a small flight of five steps to a tiny apartment.

Aggie's apartment was furnished quite sparsely. There were none of the grandmotherly touches of old framed pictures, afghans and lace tablecloths. Instead, there was an array of casual decor, a floor devoid of carpeting of any kind and scattered pieces of art that had been fashioned from driftwood and sea rocks. The only picture in the room was an angry rendition of the sea, giving the wall an almost foreboding look. Catching Jill staring at it, Aggie clucked like a chicken over a brood of chicks she was particularly fond of. "Logan painted that for me," she said with the pride of ownership, "and I guess it's just about my favorite thing in the whole world."

"It takes my breath away," Jill said honestly as she admired the turbulent sea scene.

"Haven't you ever seen any of his work in the galleries in New York?" Aggie asked. "He's had showings all over the country."

Patting Jill's hand in a motherly fashion, Aggie reached out to adjust the picture from its crooked stance on the wall. "You will soon enough, my dear. He's got a showing coming up in Boston in less than a month's time, and if it's the success it promises to be, he'll sign a contract for a display in a Paris gallery."

Jill had tried to act enthusiastic, but she found herself itching to get back to her cabin. The day's events were beginning to take their toll, and she craved the chance to stretch out on a real bed.

"You look about done in. That's what this country fresh air does for you. Why don't you go back to your cabin now and catch a few winks of sleep? I'll come and get you when it's time for dinner, or else I'll send Doozey to wake you. We'll have lots of time to talk before I leave for Seattle."

Jill was tired. A short catnap would work wonders. "I think I'll do just that. I'm going to help you with the cleanup after dinner. Mr. Matthews . . . ah . . . suggested it when he left Briar Cottage."

"Did he, now?" Aggie's eyes twinkled. "More like he ordered you to do it. Logan is a great one for issuing orders and getting people to obey them. Funny how no one ever defies him. Makes a body wonder somehow how he does it. Scat now. I have to get back to my cooking."

Jill laughed. She liked the talkative older woman. Liked her a lot. A pity she was going away. Who would be her ally, her confidant, when she was gone? Doozey, who else? Besides, the setter couldn't take sides.

Coming back to Briar Cottage alone was like seeing it for the first time. She hadn't even opened the checkered curtains.

Her fantasies left her totally unprepared

for reality, and the moment the parlor light was switched on, Jill felt as though she had committed highway robbery. The front room was the largest, accommodating a brass bed with a homey, star-stitched quilt and a pair of lace-encased pillows. A few feet from the end of the bed was a round breakfast table, covered with a checkered tablecloth. Two wire-backed chairs were pushed up against it, a ready invitation for an impromptu snack. Jill was reminded of her uneaten avocado sandwich. The bathroom was complete with a pull-chain commode and a bathtub that boasted clawed feet and ornate silver fixtures; regrettably, neither worked.

Jill could only nod her approval silently, thanking the fates for guiding her car down that long, seldom-used road.

Jill whirled about the room, allowing herself a contented sigh. Eyeing the bed, she knew that she was too wound up to consider sleep even though she was tired. Slipping on a sweater, she latched the door behind her and set off in the direction she supposed would most quickly lead her to the sea. The short walk around the compound had just been her way of acquainting herself with her immediate surroundings. This walk, her second of the day, was to buoy her spirits, to revitalize herself in some way.

The terrain was mostly mottled with patches of the type of beach grass found along most beaches in the area. It wasn't long before she hit the dunes, clambering up even the steepest of them in a promise to herself that she wouldn't head back until she had caught her first glimpse of the sea. The beach stretched out in a flat, infinite landscape, hypnotizing Jill as the granules of sand caught the orange glow of a fast-approaching sunset. Spotting a formation of rocks a few hundred yards ahead of her, Jill made that her goal. Selecting one of the largest, more contoured boulders, she sat down and positioned herself so she could absorb the view at her leisure.

The sun bounced along the horizon, hanging for a moment before sliding into the sea. A low sound heralded its descent, and Jill sat up abruptly, convinced that the sounds she was hearing were not entirely those of nature. Her suspicion gave way to conviction as the muted sounds of a song reached her ears. She couldn't decipher the words, but the melody haunted her. The whispering cries of scattered sands drew her attention to a spot a few yards away. There, perched on the sands, was an easel with a man beside it dismantling his canvas and storing his brushes in a satchel he had slung over one shoulder. Logan Matthews preferred late-afternoon light in his efforts to find inspiration for his painting.

Jill contemplated speaking, for surely he would hear her across such a short distance. But something made her remain silent. In the next instant she was glad she had followed her instincts, for as the man turned his back on the sea his face was as angry as the seascape in Aggie's room. Jill fought to hold back her gasp of something akin to fear. Never in her life had she seen such stormy emotions and yet there was a shadow of pain beneath it all. But he had been so warm, so contented-looking, when he was with the frolicking Irish setter.

Quietly, Jill withdrew. She made her way back to Briar Cottage with her thoughts in a turmoil. Logan Matthews was a man to be reckoned with. A man of contradictions, as changeable as the sea itself — tranquil one moment and turbulent the next with emotions whipped to a frothy fever.

Aggie was as good as her word. Promptly at three minutes to six Doozey whined outside the cottage door. Jill gathered up her sweater and dutifully followed the dog across the compound. Sounds of laughter and easy camaraderie greeted her as she entered the door. One-on-one introductions were made, with Jill saying her name over and over. No one asked what she did. It was evident that if Logan Matthews accepted her she was all right in their eyes.

Jack De Marco was a wide-eyed, freckle-faced sculptor from Los Angeles who shook hands gently. His grin was infectious as he released Jill's hand and turned her over to Aaron Michaelson, who claimed to be the best photographer on the East Coast. It wasn't just his opinion, he went on to say; *Life* magazine backed him up one hundred percent. Pat Laird the journalist shook Jill's hand firmly and then warmly embraced her. "Nice to see a fellow female. I've been feeling slightly outnumbered around here with all these guys. Welcome aboard, or whatever it is you say in the creative world."

They accepted her completely and Jill felt right at home amidst the busy chatter as they waited for the food to be brought to their table.

Jill settled herself in a round captain's chair and waited to be served. Thick bowls of tantalizing clam chowder were set down on the table along with a heaping plate of crusty bread. Round scoops of golden butter, sitting in a pyramid, graced the middle of the red checkered cloth. Jill binged with the rest of her table companions. She felt stuffed when the last drop of the creamy chowder slipped down her throat. She was further amazed when a heaping platter of fried chicken and a gigantic bowl of salad appeared. Jill groaned as did the others. They fell to it, murmuring their approval of Aggie's expertise in the kitchen.

No sooner were the dinner plates set aside than the biggest slices of pie Jill had ever seen were placed in the center of the table. "Homemade ice cream," Aggie announced. "I made it myself last night. Eat up."

More groans as the diners attacked the luscious pie and creamy ice cream. There were choruses of, "I'll have to run for two hours tonight," "I'll have to do two hundred sit-ups instead of one hundred," and other general comments about waistlines.

Out of the corner of her eye Jill noticed Logan Matthews staring at her. There seemed to be an amused glint in his eyes. He was testing her. She knew it and so did Logan. And from the grinning faces of the others they knew it too. He knew she couldn't cook like this. She wasn't a seasoned salt like Aggie. Jill's back straightened. He wanted her to fall flat on her face so he could say, I told you so. He was the kind of man who would step over her when she did fall and go about his business. After all, she had seen that angry face by the water. She shivered as she looked around the dining hall.

Jill decided she would give her stay at the colony her best shot, and if that didn't work, she would leave. At that point it would matter little if Logan wanted the money or not. Her best shot. "Male chauvinist," she muttered to herself as her companions scraped back their chairs in preparation for the long evening of athletics ahead. Jill seriously doubted if any of them would make good on their promises to work out later. Speaking strictly for herself, the kitchen duty she was assigned would be all she could handle.

It was an exhausting two hours. The crockery seemed to weigh a ton. Jill lost track of the number of trips she made from the dining room to the makeshift kitchen with its cold-water sink.

She was drying the last piece of silver with a soaking dish towel when Logan motioned for her to meet him outside. Aggie gave her a sly wink and set about stacking the dishes on the shelves. "Go ahead, honey, you're the prettiest thing Logan has seen in a long time. Enjoy the evening. Jill?"

It was a question and Jill waited.

"Jill, Logan is a hard man to figure out. He might seem callous and hard to some people when he's really not that way at all. He's been hurt to the core and doesn't want to be put in that position again. I heard the two of you sniping away at each other this afternoon. Voices carry across the compound, remember that. He's a man."

Outside, the air was chill, almost cold; tastes of the coming winter were sharp in the night. Jill shivered slightly, pulling her sweater closely around her shoulders. "Brrr . . . gets cold early here."

"Here?" Logan questioned. "Where's there?"

"Oh, the southern tip of New Jersey. I suppose it's cold enough there right now, but this is different."

"Perhaps it's being so close to the ocean. The air is damper, you feel the cold more."

"No, that's not it," she told him quietly. "I've lived near the ocean all my life. We do have a seashore in Jersey, you know. It's just different here — like a Currier and Ives painting about to be drawn. It's like expecting the sweet taste of maple syrup before you open the bottle."

"I like that, what you just said. Perhaps you'll make a writer after all."

Their steps were taking them in the direction of Briar Cottage, and somehow Jill felt like a girl being walked home from school, only Logan wasn't carrying her books. She wasn't exactly looking forward to the next morning and latrine duty, as he called it. During the cleanup after dinner, she had seriously considered leaving Mill Valley. Surely, there must be someplace she could stay where she wouldn't be expected to work so hard. At this point, and with all the thinking she had to do, she would be more than willing to pay her way someplace where she could get her thoughts and feelings together.

Not that she was lazy, far from it, but seeing the feast Aggie had set before them that evening had scared the dickens out of her. There was no way she could ever hope to equal that good home cooking, and she was dreading the thought of portending failure.

She could leave and, more than likely, she *should* leave. But walking under the trees with the brine of the ocean in the air and the peace . . . Jill knew without a doubt that she would stay, must stay. She felt inexplicably drawn to Mill Valley and strangely curious about the enigma that was Logan Matthews.

"Penny . . ."

"What? Oh, my thoughts. I was thinking how peaceful it is here."

Logan nodded, agreeing.

"There's a beauty here, a kind of healing."

"Healing? Funny you should call it that."

The tone of his voice deepened; there was a sadness, a mournful quality, in his words, and Jill believed he was thinking of his own broken romance.

They continued their walk until the dim light of her cottage was visible through the trees. Doozey barked and scampered on ahead, expecting his master and Jill to follow him to the cottage.

"I'll leave you here," Logan told her. "Doozey will see you the rest of the way."

Again, that mournful note in his voice. Was he trying to tell her that he was sorry he had put her in the cottage that had been closed ever since the girl he loved ran out on him? Did his mention of Doozey remind him that he and his setter had walked this trail to the cottage many times — happier times?

"Good night, Logan," Jill heard herself say, looking up into his handsome face, seeing pain in his eyes.

Suddenly, without warning, he scooped her into his arms. His mouth took hers, searing her lips with his own. His arms were strong, drawing her close, holding her fast, preventing her escape. And Jill clung to him, needing him, wanting to make him believe that she was a woman, a woman and worthy of love. She demanded that he erase all thoughts of Deke's rejection from her mind, her heart.

Logan's embrace tightened. His lips moved over hers, evoking a never-before-imagined emotion from deep within her. A sound formed in her throat and was silenced by his kiss. His arms were bands of steel, holding her fast, pressing her against him, making her aware of his masculinity, his dominance.

Doozey was howling; Logan was muttering something, something she couldn't understand. As quickly as he had seized her, he set her free, making her feel as though her legs would buckle under and she would fall to the crazily whirling ground.

His hands reached out to steady her, his hands warm against her chilled flesh. For an instant she thought he was going to take her in his arms again. Instead, he stared at her, a frown creasing his brow, his dark hair falling over his forehead. It was his mouth that fascinated her and held her attention. It was grim, tight with sorrow, taut with rage.

Abruptly, he turned on his heel and left her alone beneath the trees with only the light from her cottage to show the way.

Jill awoke early the next morning, her mind holding groggy images of the day before. She could remember coming back across the dunes, having waited long after Logan left with his easel.

Propelled by thoughts of a hearty plate of bacon and eggs, Jill rolled off the bed, wrapping the quilt around her as a makeshift robe. The room was unbearably cold, the morning breezes from the sea curling under the door and seeping through every affordable entrance the cabin offered. Jill remembered with a groan that breakfast was only a fantasy until she could get to the dining hall.

Gritting her teeth to try to control their chattering, Jill tossed the quilt back onto the end of the bed. Undressing as fast as she could, she decided to wear one of the blouses she had purchased in town, along with the unusual skirt that somehow appealed to her more every time she looked at it. Completing the effect with her new cork-colored boots, she then covered her chill-bumped arms with the warm comfort of her sweater.

In an action prodded more by duty than choice, Jill sorted through the confusion in her tote bag to try to locate the postcards that she had bought. Choosing a rather dated photograph of Mill Valley's main street, slashed across the middle with a furled banner that read Welcome to Mill Valley, Jill poised her hand over the blank message area on the back, not sure just what to say or how to say it. Something that the elderly woman by the roadside had said to her jumped into her mind, and she wrote to Nancy Evans:

> Kidnapped by gypsies! Caravan camped out at Woodmeire Cottages on the outskirts of town.
>
> Jill

Jill glanced at her watch. She would watch the sun come up. A chilling, bracing walk would do her a world of good. She could even jog and try to work off some of Aggie's dinner from the night before. And she could try to put the memory of Logan's kiss behind her, try to put from her mind the memory of how his arms felt around her.

Try. It was like giving her stay here her best shot. All she could do was try.

Her legs felt like Jell-O as she slid them into her skirt. Just thinking of the handsome man was turning her weak-kneed and silly. No doubt there was even a stupid look on her face in the bargain. Aggie had been so right. Never in her life had she been kissed so soundly, so thoroughly. What all the romantic magazines said was true. The earth did tilt, the fireworks did shower the heavens. Deke had told her bells would ring *after* marriage, but Logan Matthews had made them ring with his first kiss. Deke had lied. She should hold her rioting emotions in check, Jill cautioned herself. She should be wary of Logan and of all men. It was so soon since she had been disappointed, humiliated. But all that seemed to be a different time, a different place. Also, it was true that nothing could perk up a battered ego like the attention of a new man, especially an exciting man like Logan Matthews. And the fact that Logan could excite her and salve her pride proved to Jill that whatever she had felt for Deke, it had not been love.

Satisfied that she had fulfilled her obligation with the postcards, Jill laid them on the table by the front door to be mailed sometime in the future.

Closing the door behind her, she found herself wondering if Logan Matthews was awake or slaving artistically over a blank canvas. Scolding herself for allowing her thoughts to be occupied by the man, Jill marched across the tiny porch and down the steps to the road. The sound of an engine barreling down the dirt road that led to her cottage caught her ear. The car definitely needed a tune-up. She looked up just in time to see a baby-blue Porsche roar past, skid to a stop and then race backward and come to a grinding, screeching halt within inches of where she was standing.

Jill stood transfixed as a tall, redheaded woman slid out of the car. The woman oozed sophistication. Her clothes were obviously of designer quality, and Jill could almost swear that her long legs boasted the luxury of real silk stockings. A single golden chain around her throat matched the belt about her tiny waist that accentuated the jade material of her dress. Her hair bounced in a style that Jill regarded with envy; a pair of sunglasses were pushed up on her head.

The woman was out of the car and fishing in her bag for what was obviously a key. Jill said nothing but watched as she then leaned over to take a petit-point bag from the bucket seat on the passenger side of the sports car. With no wasted motion she walked up the steps and fitted her key into the lock. She showed no surprise when the door opened to her touch. Puzzled, Jill followed her into Briar Cottage.

"I know this is going to sound odd, but what are you doing in my cottage?" Jill demanded.

The woman's perfectly manicured eyebrows rose into a graceful arch. "Your cottage?" She made the words sound obscene.

"Yes, my cottage. I'm staying here. I arrived yesterday and Mr. Matthews himself brought me over here. Where I come from, we don't walk into other people's lodgings without knocking. Who are you and what do you want?"

The woman laughed. It was a musical tinkle of a sound that chilled Jill to the very bone.

"I am Stacey Phillips." She made it sound important, as if she were some sort of celebrity.

"I'm Jill Barton, but that still doesn't tell me what you're doing in my cottage." Jill hoped her voice was as firm-sounding as she intended.

Stacey Phillips laughed again.

"Darling, I have a key. See!"

Jill saw the single key hanging from an expensive Gucci chain and wanted to die on the spot.

"This," she said, motioning her hand around the small cottage, "is mine. The key says it's mine. As to what I want, it's simple. I want Logan Matthews. Now, Miss whatever-your-name-is, get your things out of here. Immediately. I'll be staying here from now on."

Jill was thunderstruck. This couldn't be happening to her, it just couldn't. What was she to do? Where should she go? Aggie. Aggie would know what to do.

Squaring her shoulders, Jill gathered her belongings together and stuffed them into her carryall and tote bag. She looked around to see if she had forgotten anything. Satisfied, she stared at Stacey Phillips for a moment. She must be the woman that Aggie had told her about. Jill's stomach lurched and then settled down. Stacey was as beautiful as Logan was handsome. They must make a handsome couple, Jill thought sourly.

Dejectedly, Jill tossed her belongings into the back of her car and then trudged across to the Cape Cod house and Aggie.

Aggie turned from her stance in front of the stove.

"I saw the car," she said sourly. "Expect

Logan heard it too. What are you doing here so early?"

"I've just been tossed out of Briar Cottage. She had a key on a Gucci chain and said Briar Cottage was hers. She also told me she wanted Logan Matthews. I can only believe she meant it. That's why I'm standing here. Can I help you?"

"You sure can. Start spooning out the jam into those little dishes. You can bunk in with me. I've got twin beds in my room. Come the weekend, you'll have the whole place to yourself. That solves two problems. Now all we have to do is figure out what *she's* doing here."

Aggie's voice was full of disgust as she turned the long strips of bacon on the grill.

"She said she came for Logan," Jill said with a catch in her throat.

"She probably came because of business. I'm not saying she doesn't want Logan. I'm sure she does. Miss Phillips works in an art gallery in New York. Her father is the one who arranges for all of Logan's showings. Wouldn't surprise me a bit if she turned out to be the one who is going to arrange and handle Logan's Paris show."

"Will Logan be going to Paris, do you think?" Jill asked in a small voice.

Aggie grimaced. "Probably," she said

curtly. “She’s here, in the front parlor. Listen,” Aggie commanded.

“I can’t eavesdrop,” Jill protested.

“Well, I can. I have no scruples when it comes to Logan. I love him like he was my own son. Here, you watch the bacon.”

Aggie tiptoed over to the door leading to Logan’s dining room and stood with her ear pressed against the white panel. Jill felt sick.

The loud voices reached her ears. She listened, forgetting her rules against eavesdropping.

Four

"Stacey! What are you doing here? Whatever it is, forget about it. I told you a year ago that I would only do business with your father. We have nothing to say to each other."

"You're a fool, Logan. Haven't you heard? My father is in the south of France recuperating from a coronary. I'm in charge of the gallery. I had my secretary write you three separate letters, all of which you ignored. I made this trip up here purposely to talk to you. It's time we mended fences. Logan, I'm sorry about the way I left you, but —"

"Spare me, Stacey. I'm busy. It's almost breakfast time. If you recall, we do things on a schedule around here. Now that you're here, I can see that I'll have to make arrangements for you."

"Don't worry your head about a thing. I made my arrangements. I moved into Briar Cottage a few moments ago. And yes, darling, I recall many, many moments, all of them ecstatically happy, with you at Briar Cottage."

Jill's eyes popped open as her gaze met Aggie's forlorn look.

"You what? I assigned that cottage yesterday —"

"That's what she said when she left. Possession, darling . . ."

Jill could just imagine the stunning Stacey waving her Gucci key chain with the key to Briar Cottage under Logan's nose.

"You can just move yourself right back out. You can stay in the Wynde Cottage. You can't come here and upset the routine I've established. I won't have it. You left once. Coming back entitles you to nothing but what I choose to give you. Move to Wynde Cottage!"

"Not on your life. I like Briar Cottage. It holds too many memories for me to give it up to some slip of a girl in tacky denim. We have a contract, Logan. A contract that you signed. It's true that you signed it with my father, but I now have his power of attorney. You and I will be working together. In order for us to have a harmonious relationship I will stay at Briar Cottage where I am comfortable."

"She's got him over a barrel," Aggie hissed.

Jill nodded mutely.

"I don't need you to advise me on my

legal rights. I'm an attorney, remember?" Logan snapped.

"Darling, as if I could ever forget." Her voice was suddenly cold and hard, just like Logan's. "You have a contract with my gallery, and I plan to see that you live up to it. To the letter! How do you expect me to plan anything if I'm not allowed to be involved with the pieces you're doing? It's convenient for me, Logan."

"And forget about the girl as long as you get what you want, right, Stacey?" Logan thundered. Not waiting for any response, he continued. "Pieces! Is that what you think art is? So many 'pieces' to be delivered by a set date? You can't time creativity, Stacey. You know nothing and care nothing about art aside from its monetary values."

"Honestly," Stacey retorted, "why I put up with your temperament . . ."

"Because it makes you money," Logan barked. "It enables you to whiz around in your fancy Porsche and it got you into that exclusive country club you always wanted to drag me to. Stacey, you wouldn't know how to live any other way."

"Temper, temper, Logan," Stacey cooed.

"Aggie!"

It was another bark, a demand for immediate attention. The door to the kitchen slammed open, almost knocking Aggie from her eavesdropping position. Logan's eyes took in the scene and his jaw tightened.

"Evidently, you heard."

If he was surprised to see Jill, he said nothing. Jill turned away, unable to meet his angry gaze. The hot bacon grease hissed and sputtered. Jill sniffed as she lifted the strips of bacon and laid them on several layers of thick paper towels to drain.

"Aggie?"

"Yes, Logan," Aggie said in a motherly tone.

"I want you to take —"

"I already told Jill she could bunk in with me and when I leave on the weekend, she can have the room to herself. I figured that was what you would want."

A look of relief washed over Logan's face. "What would I do without you, Aggie?" was all he said as he left the kitchen.

"Aggie, I've been thinking," Jill said as she put the finishing touches to one of the heavy trays. "Maybe I should stay in the Wynde Cottage till you leave. It's not that I don't want to stay with you, it's just that I want to be alone to do some thinking. I hope you don't mind. I thought I might wander by the cottage after breakfast and take a look. If I change my mind, is your offer still open?"

"Of course." There was genuine affection in Aggie's voice as she too finished up another of the heavily laden trays. She looked around to see if she had forgotten anything.

"Now watch, Jill, this is how it works."

She gave a bell hanging near the ancient stove a long pull. The sound was deafening. Within minutes Jack and Aaron whizzed through the door and literally raced to the dining hall, the heavy trays extended in front of them.

"I get the coffee urn ready the night before, and the first person in the dining hall plugs it in. We have a generator over there, did you know that?"

Jill shook her head.

The photographer and the sculptor were back for the second load. Aggie handed Jill a basket holding the breakfast rolls, and she herself carried two jugs of orange juice.

"That about does it. You'll see, everything will be piping hot when we sit down. Want to know the secret?" Again, Jill nodded. "I keep the plates warming in the oven."

She would never remember all of this, Jill thought morosely as she trudged behind Aggie.

The breakfast atmosphere was a repeat of dinner the night before. The only exception was that Logan Matthews was not in attendance. Nor was Stacey Phillips.

The washing and cleaning up were completed by nine o'clock.

"Is there anything else you have for me to do, Aggie? No? Show me where the bath . . . the latrines are. That's my job, you know. I have to clean them. I almost forgot, what with Miss Phillips arriving and all. Even Mr. Matthews didn't chew me out. I expected he would. I suppose he forgot too."

Aggie nodded sagely. "Everything you'll need is in the cupboard inside. It's really no big mess. Most of the guests are respectful of each other and try to leave the bathrooms clean. Once in a while we get a messy one like Miss Phillips. She smears the place from one end to the other, and when she comes out she looks as though she stepped off a magazine page. What people don't see is the mess she leaves behind. All the cottages have bathrooms, but Logan was running into such expense with the separate drains, he had all the plumbing turned off a couple of years ago. Now we have this one community room, and it does seem to work better. Logan said this was a communal kind of living and everyone was to share. I think he was right. At the time I wasn't all that hepped up on the idea, but now I like it just fine. You will too after you get used to it. The left side is for the ladies, right side for men."

"Okay, Aggie. Thanks for everything. It's okay, then, if I move into Wynde Cottage till you leave? Do you think I should tell Mr. Matthews?"

"It will be all right. I'll tell him myself. I have to go into town for some supplies. That is, if that confounded pickup is working."

Jill's ears perked up. "What's wrong with the pickup?"

"Engines are a mystery to me. All I know is it grinds and then stalls. Makes me crazy is what it does. I spoke to Logan about it and he said he would take a look at it the first chance he got. That was near three weeks ago, and he still hasn't gotten around to it. I just cross my fingers each time I get into it."

"Want me to take a look at it?" Jill asked hopefully.

"Honey, you can look at it all you want. If you like dirty old engines, I guess it can't hurt anything."

There was hope in the older woman's voice when she asked suddenly, "Jill, do you know anything about engines, or do you just like to look at them?"

Jill grinned. "A little bit of both. Let's take a look."

Aggie seated herself behind the wheel and waited to do Jill's bidding.

"Again, Aggie. Start it up again. Okay, I see what it is. Now start it."

Aggie turned the key and grinned from ear to ear. "What did you do to it?" she asked in amazement.

Jill withdrew her head, her face wearing a matching grin.

"Oh, I just . . ."

"Yes, I'd be interested in hearing what you did. This truck hasn't worked right in months," Logan Matthews said quietly.

"Well, this old engine is purring like a kitten, and it only took her two hours. Isn't it amazing, Logan?"

Jill looked sheepish. Her hands were full of grease and her shirt had a streak of grease which resembled a streak of lightning running from the neckline to her waist.

"I know I didn't clean the bath . . . latrines yet. But Aggie said she wanted to go into town, so I thought . . . what I mean is, I wanted to . . ." Seeing Logan's steely eyes, she wiped her hands on her jeans and backed off several steps. "I'm going to do it now. Right now," she said emphatically. "Go easy on the choke, Aggie, when you start off," she called over her shoulder.

Jill set about making herself presentable.

Then she cleaned the bathrooms. Her mother would have been hard pressed to find fault with the completed job. Now she was on her own. Now she could do whatever it was she wanted to do. She would move into Wynde Cottage and then go for another long walk.

Might as well drive her car to the cottage and save herself a trip later. Besides, her bags were in the back seat. No point in making more work for herself.

Even though she felt tired, Jill decided to give the cabin a complete cleaning. The only vixen that had escaped Aggie's scouring hand was dust. A peppery film of it layered almost everything, and Jill hummed silently to herself as she set about a campaign to banish it from existence.

The hours passed swiftly, Jill stopping only long enough to snack on a chocolate bar and some peanuts in her handbag.

Deciding to wash off the grime that she had accumulated on her person during her frenzied housecleaning, Jill headed for the sanitation station. She grinned as she discovered that Aggie had thought of every pleasure; a tall canister of bath oil sat hidden behind a fold of the shower curtain. Dumping an ample amount into the one tub, Jill turned on the tap, watching the crystals dissolve into a frothy pink foam. Stripping quickly, she stepped into the inviting warmth and leaned back. The water continued to gush forth, massaging her feet in a rhythmic whirlpool. She closed her eyes, moaning in satisfaction as she felt the water inch up across her body, waiting until it almost reached her chin before she lifted one foot and turned off the spout with her toes.

Daydreaming, Jill began to sing as she soaped her arms and shoulders. When she cleaned, she had failed to see something that now caught her eye. Wedged beneath the sink sat a trunk, the type Jill thought belonged more in an attic. Ignoring her Pandora pleadings, Jill tried to persuade herself that Aggie had probably stocked the case with bathroom supplies. Lecturing herself for feeling snoopy, Jill rinsed off and grabbed the fleecy towel that hung on a rack beside the sink. Without bothering to dress first, she pulled the trunk out to the middle of the bathroom floor. It was too heavy to hold just towels and washcloths, and Jill found herself stifling a giggle of excitement as she lifted the lid. Books! The entire box was filled with books. Greedily devouring the titles, Jill knew she had found a treasure store that would comfort her through many a long, lonely night. Selecting one of the largest bound treasures, Jill read the title out loud: "*A Study of Gothic Architecture.*" Flipping through the gold-edged pages, Jill marveled over the beautiful illustrations that had been etched in pen and ink. Knowing that she would want time to examine each page one by one, she laid the book aside and secreted the rest of the bounty back in its hiding place.

Lunch seemed the furthest thing from her mind as Jill settled down at the table in the sitting room of Wynde Cottage. A quick search for the Irish setter had found him snoozing beneath her bed, his ears twitching as though his dreams had carried him across the dunes in pursuit of a gull.

It was late afternoon before Jill closed the book and paid heed to the dog's whining. Nature bidding, she realized when he trotted to the door and barked assertively. Feeling the need to stretch her legs herself, Jill joined the animal as it bounded out toward the beach.

The wind was brisk and the surf was up as Jill and Doozey romped up to their knees in the surprisingly warm water. Gulls swooped and screamed, keeping them company during their search for pretty shells.

Today there was no sign of Logan on the beach, and with a pang Jill considered that he was probably with the fiery-haired Stacey Phillips. From what she had heard of the argument between them that morning it had seemed that Stacey was trying to apologize but that Logan kept interrupting her. Perhaps by this time they had kissed and made up. Stacey Phillips looked to be the kind of woman who always got what she was after, and her female instinct told Jill that Miss Phillips was after Logan.

Knowing by the low growl in her stomach that it was close to dinnertime, she whistled for Doozey and followed him back to the main house where Aggie was cooking. Jill felt revived by her walk, and although her assigned chores didn't require her working the dinner hour, she decided she would give a hand in helping the older woman get the meal on the table and cleared away.

"Honestly, Doozey, I'll never know how Aggie does it! Even with my help it took almost two hours to get everything cleared away last night." She groaned inwardly. How many hours would it take her to do Aggie's job all alone?

All through dinner, Jill kept a wary eye on Logan's empty chair. Miss Phillips also was missing from the dinner table. He had probably taken her to some posh restaurant, she thought. Aggie's home cooking isn't good enough for our resident art dealer.

Still, even with all the commotion and camaraderie at the table, Jill felt Logan's absence. "This is silly," she scolded herself, pushing away her half-eaten dinner. "You've only known the man for a day, and yet you lose your appetite because you miss him!"

Too tired from her long day to consider reading herself to sleep, Jill readied herself for bed. Having had little else to choose from in her luggage that was appropriate for sleeping other than filmy, whisper-soft negligees, she hastily allowed the peach-colored silk to slide over her body. Grimacing as she looked at herself in the mirror, she felt a dull pang of sorrow. This nightie was a part of her trousseau and she had chosen it with the thought of pleasing Deke. Stiffening her upper lip and pushing aside her regrets, she admitted that the nightgown still pleased *her,* and that was really all that mattered.

Fastening the little satin ribbon at the plunging neckline, she saw how revealing the nightie was as it hugged the soft curves of her figure and fell with subtle allure to her ankles.

Crawling beneath the covers, she realized with a laugh that she hadn't thought of Deke all day, until just this minute. Surely, that proved something. Weren't you supposed to constantly think about the someone you loved?

Ignoring her own question, she turned on her side, inviting sleep. She was lost somewhere between dozing and deep slumber when a noise from outside made her eyes flash open. She could swear someone was walking by her cottage. Holding her breath to make her hearing more acute, Jill waited for the sound to come again.

"Doozey!" came a call, making Jill bolt upright in bed.

"Doozey! Where are you, dog?"

This last demand was followed by the whistling of a master for his dog. Lying back against her pillow, Jill found herself smiling and admitted that it was because Logan Matthews was back in the compound and thinking of his dog, not Miss Phillips.

Drifting back into a light sleep, she was again awakened, this time by an insistent scratching on the front door.

Forcing herself to climb out from beneath the warm covers, Jill went to investigate. The source of the disturbance took immediate insult at being ignored and, with a resounding thud, pitched itself against the bottom half of the door. Peering out from behind the curtains hanging from the small window beside the door, Jill spied a wagging red tail.

The greeting Doozey gave her when she opened the door always bowled her over, and she could see that the poor beast was hungry for affection. At first, the dog seemed to be content to languish against her legs, his eyes radiant pools of gratitude as she stroked his coat and cooed to him. Jill laughed as his nose poked around the air, sniffing out the origin of her snack of hours ago.

"You big baby," she teased, "hoping for an invitation to share my snack? You're too late; it's all gone."

The dog barked, issuing an affirmative to Jill's question.

"Come on, I suppose I can find a Chunky bar for you."

Leaning back in the cottage's one chair, she watched in fascination as the setter began to dine on his chocolate. She had expected him to gulp down the offering in one voracious bite. Instead, he savored it a morsel at a time, showing Jill he was a dog gifted with class.

"Doozey! Where are you?" a hushed voice demanded just outside the cottage. Logan Matthews.

"You'd better get going, Doozey. Your

master seems to be in a vile mood," she told her guest as she opened the door and tried to shove him out.

"So this is where you've gotten to," Logan said sternly, surprising both girl and dog to find him right outside the door. "You get home now!"

Doozey whimpered and tried to hide himself behind Jill's legs.

"Don't talk to him that way!" she scolded the artist. "It's little wonder the poor creature is afraid to go with you. Look at him!" she pointed to Doozey, who was now crouching fearfully, his wet black nose pressed between her bare feet.

"Don't let him fool you, Jill. He's an Academy-Award-winning actor, believe me."

"The poor baby was starved and came begging for food," she argued. "Don't you ever feed your pets, Mr. Matthews?"

Somehow she couldn't tell this man that she didn't believe it was food Doozey was looking for but affection. Jill couldn't bring herself to betray the dog that way. Logan Matthews wasn't a man who would yield to begging for his favor.

"The 'poor dog,' as you call him, had a very fine dinner," he said coldly, penetrating her with a steely glance.

"There's more to life than just food, you know. Doozey was lonely for affection." She gulped. She had said it. Darn, darn. . . .

"We all need affection, Miss Barton." His voice had become husky, stealing her attention away from Doozey to himself. "Do you dole it out in large doses as you do candy?"

She could see that his eyes had noticed the Chunky bar wrapper in her hand. Suddenly, she was aware of the filmy nightgown she was wearing. If Logan had seen the candy wrapper in her hand, what else could he see? A rush of heat warmed her body, seeming to make it glow against the darkness outside. A sudden chill made her shiver — or was it just his cold blue eyes flicking over her body?

"You'll catch your death," he told her, seeing her shiver. "Get inside and I'll haul Doozey out of there."

His hands closed over her shoulders as he led her into the cottage and closed the door behind him. Somehow those strong fingers never released their grip. Somehow they gathered her close to him and held her in an embrace.

Another shudder took its hold, and this time Jill was certain it wasn't from the cold. It was from the nearness of him, the strength of him. With a creeping dismay, Jill realized how remote this cottage was from the rest of the compound and how alone she was with Logan. The size of his body made her feel even more defenseless.

"You'd better take your dog and go," Jill told him, her voice becoming a whisper.

She pulled out of his grasp, backing away, ready to run if she had to. His strong hands bit into her upper arms and bands of steel made her his prisoner. She struggled helplessly against his strength. His face was carved into bitter lines. His mouth was hard and unyielding as he brought it closer to hers and finally covered her mouth in a demanding kiss.

Against her will, her lips parted beneath his, giving themselves up to his demand, yielding to his searching hunger. She was swept up in a haze of confusion, her mind directing her one way and her body betraying her to another.

Her body was molded against his closer, closer, as his lips became more demanding. His hands made excursions along her spine, heightening her response. Nothing stood between his hand and her flesh other than a film of silk. A riot of emotions raced through her. She had never been kissed this way, had never responded this way. Fires were ignited deep within her being, revealing hidden recesses of sensuality that had never made themselves known to her before.

Where a moment ago she had tried to escape his embrace, she was now trapped in the throes of her own desire. She felt herself melt against him, molding herself to him, seeking to fill a hunger, a yearning, that this man created in her.

Beyond reason or thought, she knew he was picking her up and carrying her to the bed, never lifting his mouth from hers. She was dimly aware of his weight beside her on the covers. Her heart pounded in rhythms without pattern, beating against her breast, just beneath the touch of his fingers grazing over the sheer silk and her warm flesh. Rapturous sensations became her world, as though she had never known any other. Fulfillment beckoned to her across miles and miles of fleeting caresses and burning kisses. His hands left burning trails on her body, and she offered herself to him. All rational thought ceased. Only thoughts of Logan persisted in penetrating the fog that surrounded her.

His teasing lips were searching, seeking, finding. His gentle hands demanded, stroked, worshiped. His warm body was pressing, covering, shielding. Smoldering senses, all of them her own yet alien to her, begged for the touch and kiss of this man, Logan.

An insistent whining, deep and throaty, shattered the silence. For an instant Jill believed she was the origin of those primeval sounds until a weight threw itself against the bed, breaking the ecstasy. Doozey!

Logan rose from the bed beside her and stood looking down at her.

"You have no idea what you do to a man, do you?" he asked huskily.

Without him beside her, warming her, setting fire to her senses, the air was suddenly cold, instantly chilling her. She wrapped her arms about herself to ward off the chill. Logan seemed to take it as a gesture of modesty.

"Don't ever hide yourself from me, Jill. You don't realize just how beautiful you are."

His look was almost a physical touch as it branded her body from the sleek length of her thigh where her nightgown was rucked up to the plunging V of her neckline where her breasts were full and heaving.

When he leaned toward her again, she instinctively wrapped her arms around his neck, her fingers raking through the thick, dark hair at the nape of his neck.

Instead of resuming his embrace, he

picked her up and moved her to the pillows, where he put her down again, tucking the covers around her.

"Doozey!" he called to the dog. "You stay here with Jill and watch over her for me."

He snapped his fingers and pointed to the little rag rug beside the bed. Obediently Doozey went to his designated place and rested his head on his paws.

Without another glance in Jill's direction, Logan left the cottage, snapping off the lights before he closed the door behind him.

For a long while Jill lay quietly, thinking of the man who had carried her to this bed and who had ignited passions in her that she had never known existed. Her body still felt warm from his touch and her lips felt burning and ravished. She blushed as she recalled her own wanton responses to his lovemaking.

Pulling the covers up tightly around her neck, his words buzzed through her brain.

"Don't ever hide yourself from me, Jill," he had said, his voice throbbing with urgency. "You don't know how beautiful you are."

Jill woke early and lay still, her thoughts jumbled. Perhaps she had only been dreaming. Perhaps Logan hadn't come to the cottage looking for Doozey at all, and perhaps he hadn't taken her into his arms and taught her new depths to her own sensuality.

Lightly, her fingers touched her mouth, tenderly falling upon the place where Logan's mouth had so greedily kissed her. Trailing a path down her neck to the place between her breasts, she felt a flurry of excitement bubble. "Don't hide from me. . . ." His words were spoken softly, huskily, meaningfully. She could never hide from Logan, she told herself. Just being with him, in his arms, made her completely his.

Doozey slinked from his position beside the bed and stood staring at her, bringing new color to her cheeks. Doozey! Living proof that it hadn't been a dream. It had been real — those moments alone with Logan — here on this very bed.

Doozey's impatience prevented Jill from lying back against the pillows and recalling each and every wonderful moment in Logan's arms. The dog's tail wagged furiously, accompanied by a low whine.

"I know, I know, you want out. Could you wait a few more minutes? No, huh? No time to think, is that it?"

Shivering against the morning chill, Jill climbed from her nice warm bed and opened the door for Doozey, who rushed past her barking gratitude for his freedom.

Sighing wearily, Jill closed and locked the door. She really shouldn't go back to bed. She had the bathrooms to clean and her cleaning-up chores with Aggie. Yawning widely, Jill dressed quickly, adding the heavy sweater at the last minute. She would take her bath later, after her chores.

Skirting the dense shrubbery at the entrance to the sanitation building, Jill stopped in her tracks. What was that unholy racket coming from Logan's house? She listened another minute, fully expecting Doozey to rush up and explain the disturbance.

Jill looked around. There was no one in sight and the compound seemed to still be sleeping. What was that noise? Deciding her daily chore of bathroom cleaning could wait a while longer, Jill set out for the back of the house and the ensuing racket. It was enough to wake the dead.

Aggie was trying frantically to stanch the flow of water on the back porch. It took only one quick glance on Jill's part to figure out the reason. The water pump on one of the pipes leading to the ancient washer was broken.

"I heard a loud snap, and then the water

started to rush out of the machine. I can't get near enough to the plug to turn the power off," Aggie shouted in agitation. "This infernal racket is enough to drive a body to drink. What do you think it is, Jill?"

"Where's the main fuse box?" Jill shouted back.

"Outside around the corner of the house. Now, why didn't I think of that?"

Jill trotted off and with the first rays of dawn was able to make out where the fuse box rested high on the side of the house. She turned off the power and raced back to the now quiet screened-in porch.

"Breakfast is going to be late," Aggie said fretfully as she started to wring out the mop.

"So is latrine duty!" Jill grimaced as she set about to help Aggie. "I think we'd be better off if we just swept the water out the door and down the steps instead of trying to sop it up. I'll start on breakfast while you do that. What's on the menu today?"

"We were going to have blueberry pancakes and waffles with scrambled eggs," Aggie said dejectedly. "If there's one thing Logan hates, it's to have meals served late."

"There are some things in life Mr. Logan Matthews had better get used to, and the first one is that we're having cold cereal for breakfast. If he's lucky, I might throw in some orange juice. And do you know something else? I think your boss is a slave driver expecting you to kill yourself the way you've been doing. You aren't getting younger, Aggie. You could have a stroke working the way you do," she added virtuously.

"You just might be right, Jill. I'm looking forward to this trip to Seattle in more ways than I can tell you."

"It's okay for your boss to be a patron of the arts and to indulge himself with all his rules and regulations but not at someone else's expense. I'm mad, fighting mad," Jill complained as she set about pouring milk into jugs. She looked at the clock and winced. Quickly, she gave the bell next to the side of the door a vicious yank.

Jill's tired eyes defied the residents to say a word about the trays they picked up. Deciding to go all out, she called to their retreating backs, "One word from anyone and I'll take the milk back and you'll eat it dry."

Aggie burst out laughing. "Is this what you writers call rebellion or mutiny?"

"Either/or, take your pick. Let me take a look at the machine now. Do you have a toolbox handy?"

"Right here. Next to the machine. This blasted thing is so temperamental I can't stand it anymore. If we don't get it fixed, I'll have to go into town to wash the towels."

"I have a better idea. I think we should let Mr. Matthews go into town to do the wash. Hold that flashlight a little lower, Aggie. There, you see, you need a new water pump, and the belt came off. I think we can patch it up if you have some electrical tape. Oh, oh, the piston is shot. Lower, Aggie. Maybe if I hook up . . . that's it, Aggie, now hand me that little screwdriver. What's wrong with you, Aggie? Lower, I can barely see. Okay, I got it now. Hand me the pliers. I can see it now, the macho Logan Matthews doing laundry. I bet he doesn't even know how to fold towels, and he's probably one of those guys who dries off with three. Never stops to think about who has to wash them. I'm telling you, Aggie, if I hear one peep out of him about that cold cereal, I'll . . . I'll . . . there, I got it. Whew! I didn't think I could do it there for a minute. Do you have any machine oil? Aggie, is there some reason why you aren't answering me?"

"I can give you two very good reasons right off the bat, but I doubt if you would want to hear either of them," Logan Matthews retorted. "I thought I had assigned you your duties. What are you doing inside that machine? Women's work is in the kitchen where they belong."

"You're right," Jill said, withdrawing her head from the inside of the washing machine. Deftly, she snapped down the outer rim and then closed the lid.

"About what?" Logan demanded.

"That I don't care to hear them — your two reasons. Now, if you'll excuse me, I have latrine duty, or did you forget?"

Jill hadn't formulated exactly what she expected from Logan after last night, but this definitely wasn't it! How could he behave as though she were another of his slaves, like Aggie, ready and willing to do his bidding?

Logan's eyes danced with laughter. "You certainly are a busy one, aren't you? When do you have time to write?"

"In the middle of the night," Jill answered shortly without thinking. Seeing the laughter rekindle in his gaze, she flushed hotly. His hand reached out to lift a golden curl from her cheek.

"And do you also gather research for your memoirs in the middle of the night?"

Jill's knees felt weak, barely able to hold her weight.

"I think," she stammered, "you . . . you better do something about this machine. It must have come over on the Mayflower. It works now, but for how long I can't say."

She fought for composure, hoping to change the subject . . . anything!

"Jill?"

She liked the way he said her name. It sounded so soft and feminine when it came from him. When other people said her name, it always sounded so tomboyish.

"Please, whatever it is, can't it wait till I finish the bathrooms?" she pleaded.

There was no way she wanted to hear him chastise her this morning. Why couldn't he be nice to her as he was with the others? Why did he always have to mock her?

"I want to thank you for reminding me about Aggie. I have been neglectful of her. I know how to wash clothes, and believe it or not, I folded towels when I was in the marines. If you want to be really startled, I can square bedsheets and a quarter will flip. You will also notice that there has not been one peep out of me concerning that . . . cardboard you served for breakfast. What really is amazing is that no one else complained either. What I'm trying to say, Miss Barton, is, you made your point."

Jill was stunned. She shifted from one foot to the other as she stared at him. Not trusting herself to speak, she merely nodded.

"By the way, how's the book coming?"

"Book?" Jill repeated stupidly.

His eyes were dancing again. "You know, your memoirs. *That* book."

Jill nodded. "*That* book. Fine, fine. I worked all night," she lied. She crossed her fingers as she swept through the door. Outside in the fresh morning air, she let her breath out with a long sigh.

An hour later Jill let her eyes rake the bathroom area. Spotless. It was a job well done. The chrome sparkled, the sinks glistened and the floor was squeaky clean. Deftly, she added several deodorizers and gave a final squirt of Lysol to the general area.

Aggie marched in, towel in hand. "Good job, Jill. I've never seen these bathrooms so clean. Your mother can be proud of you and the way you know how to do things."

"Thanks, Aggie. I'm going to find Doozey and go for a nice, long walk. I might even go all the way into the village and get some breakfast." She lowered her voice to a bare whisper. "I hate cereal."

Aggie laughed as she turned on the water in the tub. "Will you fetch me the new *Cosmopolitan* if it's in? I like to keep up to date on the sexy side of life."

Jill doubled over with laughter. "I'll be sure to look for it. Enjoy your bath."

* * *

By the time Jill found herself in town her stomach was rumbling. She was really hungry and would have cheerfully parted with one of her back teeth for one of Aggie's breakfasts. The sign on the one and only diner in town proclaimed it was closed on Tuesdays from October 1 through May 1. Disappointed, she picked up Aggie's copy of the slick magazine at the corner drugstore along with a cup of coffee and a Danish and headed back to the compound.

Now that it was a little warmer, she went to Wynde Cottage to remove her sweater. She was annoyed with herself for not having made her bed earlier. It was the force of habit, she supposed, for she always made her bed upon rising. Something had always grated on her about walking into the bedroom and seeing the bed unmade. It seemed sacrilegious to forgo the ritual.

Smoothing out the quilt, Jill laid it across the back of the only cozy chair in the cabin. Determined to make a lazy day of it, she put reading number one on her list. And then an entire afternoon of relaxing. Tucked inside the quilt, she would be able to stave off boredom as well as the cold.

It was while she was hanging up her

clothes that Jill first heard Doozey at her door. His announcement was entirely recognizable and she found herself weakening immediately.

She hurried over to the door to open it before he scratched it down, but her greeting for the dog died on her lips. Two feet away stood Logan Matthews dressed in a pathetic-looking turtleneck and a pair of spotted jeans.

"I was wondering if you could cook a late breakfast for Doozey and me. Aggie is loaded down with the wash and I don't want to ask her. I'm not very good in the kitchen —"

He halted abruptly, "Say, if you're busy writing, I don't want to interrupt you."

"No . . . no! What I mean is, I was just making notes. I was going to walk down to the beach today," Jill hedged, but something in Logan's eyes made her respond. "Still I can't have my good buddy going hungry, can I, Doozey?" She patted the dog affectionately and was rewarded with a big smooch.

"We're grateful, aren't we, old boy?" Logan stated. "I thought for a while we were going to have to go the day on that cold cereal. Good as it was," he hastened to explain at Jill's piercing look. "I rarely eat lunch, so I've usually eaten a hearty breakfast ever since I was a kid. . . ."

Was this *the* Logan Matthews? At a loss for words? Jill grinned; she couldn't help herself.

"Winsomeness, Mr. Matthews, does not become you. Somehow, I can't imagine you ever being a little boy. You were one, weren't you?" she asked anxiously.

"Scout's honor. My parents said I was the best boy on the block." He grinned. "Actually, we lived on a ranch in Wyoming. I was a good kid. Never got into trouble in the wide-open spaces. I broke my collarbone when I was ten, jumping off the shed roof. When I was twelve, I broke my leg bronco riding. At thirteen I fractured my elbow riding my new bike. Jenny Carpenter broke my heart when I was fourteen by going to the harvest square dance with Luke McCoy. I never fully recovered. Did I leave anything out?"

Only the part about Stacey Phillips, Jill wanted to say.

"No, I guess not; that about covers it. If you're ready, I guess I am too."

On the walk across the compound Jill was acutely aware of his nearness. She wanted to reach out and touch him, to remind him that she was real, flesh and blood, and that she had responded to him once and would again.

It seemed to take hours to finally complete the breakfast and set down a plate in front of Logan, who had sat and watched her through his lowered lids while she had worked. By this time her nerves were frazzled from his watching her that way. Each time his eyes touched her they left a burning brand, making her aware of her every movement, making her more clumsy than usual.

"Breakfast is served," she announced finally, her voice dripping sarcasm.

As he dove into his meal Logan seemed immune to the anger he had aroused in Jill.

"You know," he said matter-of-factly, waving his toast in the air as he spoke, "I find I much prefer the granola and honey bread that Nature's Bounty stocks. It toasts better."

Jill felt her heart begin pounding, her muscles tensing, and she knew it was useless to keep still any longer.

"Listen, Mr. Matthews, white bread was all we had and white bread is what you got. If you like granola and honey bread so much, see that you get yourself into town to supply it. Aggie has enough to do around here, so you can just quit demanding —"

"You find me demanding?" Logan pretended hurt.

"Yes," Jill maintained, "I certainly do."

Logan seemed puzzled by her admission

and rubbed the palms of his hands together in an unconscious gesture.

"Some people have said I was abrupt, eccentric, egotistical . . . but never demanding."

"I said it and I meant it," Jill told him emphatically.

"And you stand by your convictions, right?" His eyes held Jill's in a challenge, and she could see a glimmer in them that said she had been baited.

"And what is it you're running away from, Jill?"

Sneak attack! He was trying to find out more about her. "Running away? Who said anything about running away?" In spite of herself, her voice faltered.

"You did."

"When?"

"Your eyes, Jill," Logan said softly. "They're said to be the mirror of the soul. I'd guess your soul is running away from love."

Jill laughed, a nervous sound to her own ears.

"You couldn't be more mistaken!"

Abruptly, she rose from the table and began to clear the dishes, refusing to listen to another word. She couldn't look at him, wouldn't. His artist's eyes had seen too much already and had guessed her secret.

Five

"Goodness, Jill, I can't remember when I've had so much fun!"

A soft breeze brought a spray of sand up to tickle Jill's bare legs as she hurried over to where Aggie sat sprawled on a beach towel in tribute to the last days of Indian summer.

"I can't take all the credit," Jill said with a laugh as she sat down on the corner of the towel that Aggie had reserved for her. "This picnic was your idea."

A chuckle rumbled from deep down inside Aggie's chest as she strained forward to rub suntan oil over her legs.

"Believe it or not, Jill, I get lonely. I know I don't seem to be the clinging grandma type . . . waiting around for cards and letters that never come. There are times when being around people drives me clear up the walls. You don't come across too many honest folks these days. Most of them just care about how large a house they can latch on to . . . how many cars they can have in their garages for the neighbors to drool over. Maybe it was the way I was raised, but I just never cared for those things. Guess I was lucky when I found my Harry, because he saw things the same way. Plain and simple, that's how I like life. Sitting on the beach . . . working in Logan's garden . . . that's what makes me happy."

"You've lived here for a long time, haven't you, Aggie?"

"Seems like I was born here," the woman whispered, her eyes misting with a veil of memories. "My Harry helped Logan's pa build these cottages. They said Mill Valley was going to be put on the map by catering to artists and the like. He was right, too. Never came a season when they were alive that all the cabins weren't full. I think it was Harry that made them want to stay. He always understood their moodiness, made them feel like he was a kindred spirit. It's hard for me to believe that he's been dead almost ten years. I almost packed up and left when he died, but it would have been like running out on Harry and Logan . . . giving up on their dreams."

Afraid that she would break the spell of the past, Jill remained silent. If she hadn't come to Mill Valley and met Aggie, she would have missed something special. She realized that the brief touching of their lives would remain with her forever.

"I knew right from the first moment I saw that man that I wanted to marry him," Aggie announced finally. "And you know, Jill, when I think how close I came to passing him by, I know that him and me were just meant to be. You wouldn't know it to look at me now, but honey, I used to be just as pretty as you are. I was engaged to another man when I met Harry. The date had been set and my folks had come all the way out here from Oklahoma to see me get married. Two days before I was due in church, I suddenly knew that I didn't really love my intended. So you know what I did? I ran. I got myself a Greyhound ticket and ran. Ended up in Eureka with no job, nothing. When I called my ma, she just cried and cried, telling me I'd gone crazy. Bless her soul, she never did understand me or forgive me. Anyway, that's how I met Harry. I got a job in a diner waiting tables. Harry was the owner. All us girls used to make fun of him and his dreaming . . . telling us how he was going to have his own place with rooms for rent and a restaurant. None of us knew that he'd been salting away money for years!"

Jill felt shaken, overwhelmed by the uncanny likeness of Aggie's life to her own. "Did you ever regret your choice?"

"What?" Aggie asked blankly, still caught up in her recollecting. "Oh, you mean choosing Harry over the other fella? No, honey . . . I can honestly say that I never did. Weren't no man that could ever compare with Harry. I never met a man who could hypnotize me like he did . . . except maybe Logan. Now, there's a man that could've held a candle to my Harry. If I was thirty years younger, I'd give that Stacey Phillips a run for her money."

Jill turned, trying to hide the fact that all the color had drained from her face.

"Miss Phillips . . . you think she'll stick around?"

"I don't know," Aggie said slowly, as though trying to reach a conclusion just inches from her grasp, "but she seems to be settling in here. Makes me kind of sad, to tell the truth. She doesn't love Logan. Anyone can see that. She's just hungry for what she can get out of him. She left him once. Now she's saying they just picked up where they left off."

"Seems to be they deserve each other," Jill offered angrily. She flinched as a series of giggles erupted from the woman beside her.

"Oh, my, Jill! Don't tell me Logan has cast you under his spell!"

"I don't know what you're talking about!" Jill retorted through her teeth.

"Come on, honey," Aggie prodded. "It ain't nothing to be ashamed of. Being vulnerable and in love is what life is all about. Feel sorry for the people who don't take risks in life, Jill, because they aren't really living . . . they're merely existing."

"I don't know why you insist on saying I'm in love with Logan Matthews," Jill retorted.

"All right, Jill," Aggie relented. "I'm just telling you that you couldn't pick anyone finer. He's a good man. I've lived around him for a long time, long enough to know that despite his spells of brooding, he's a gentle and considerate human being. Look at the art he creates. A soul gifted with that much talent is bound to retreat from life now and then. Especially when all the people that are drawn to him see only what they can get . . . not what they can give."

Jill clambered to her feet, pulling her T-shirt off to reveal a salmon-pink bathing suit.

"I don't want to argue with you, Aggie. But it appears to me that the Logan

Matthews you know and the one I've had recent dealings with are two different men."

Without another word, she turned and jogged toward the water.

After managing to salvage the rest of their afternoon, Aggie and Jill walked over the dunes and headed homeward. Parting at Jill's cabin, Aggie gave Jill a smothering hug.

"Take care of yourself, Jill. Follow your heart always . . . it'll never lead you astray."

A leisurely bath to wash away the sand still holding fast to her body was Jill's top priority. Almost an hour had passed before she forced herself from the soothing balm of the water, her toes and fingers wrinkled and pink. Dressing methodically in her jeans and one of the embroidered tops, Jill loosened her hair from the strict confines of the braids she had worked earlier that morning. Her hair flowed down her back in a shimmering flaxen wave, and Jill closed her eyes as she brushed through its length until her arm ached with the effort. Selecting a book of poems by Emily Dickinson from the chest beneath the sink, Jill renewed her promise to herself of a long evening of reading.

Back in her cottage and well into the small biography that preceded the selection of poems penned by Miss Dickinson, Jill heard a telltale scratch at the door. Ignoring it, she armed herself against the inevitable whining to come. It was hopeless, for she had missed Doozey all day. Cursing herself for her weakness, Jill opened the door and saw Doozey sitting primly in the shaft of light from her lamp. A single red rose was clenched between his teeth. So taken was she with his courting that she almost neglected to see Logan Matthews standing in the shadows behind the dog. Jill felt a glow of pleasure seep through her being as she noticed his appearance. He was clean-shaven, his dark hair combed neatly. A burnished copper sweater had replaced his dingy turtleneck, and his paint-splattered jeans had been traded in for a brand-new pair. But it was what he held in both arms that made Jill laugh aloud — two bulging grocery bags, one with a truce flag fashioned from a gnarled stick and a ragged white handkerchief.

"How about it?" Logan said with a grin. "Is the apology for my nosiness accepted? I spoke out of turn when I said you were running away. Am I forgiven?"

The evening was one that Jill was convinced she would remember forever. In complete turnabout from his request for breakfast several days before, Logan settled

Jill into one of his kitchen chairs. Bowing playfully, he began to unpack the paper bags that had been filled to the top.

"My dear Miss Barton," he said as he searched the kitchen for a vase in which to deposit his surrender flag, and set it on the middle of the table, "I'm about to prepare a dinner for you that will make your dainty little taste buds stand up and holler. We'll start off with a Caesar salad and then plow into the main course."

As if to accentuate his promise, Logan held up two of the thickest steaks Jill had ever laid eyes on.

"I've got French bread and garlic butter. And chocolate chip ice cream for dessert."

Jill leaned back in her chair, her eyes dancing as she taunted him, "Actually, I prefer cherry vanilla."

Not for all the tea in China would she tell him she wasn't hungry.

It was Logan's turn to laugh and he did so heartily.

"You're a paradox, Miss Barton. One minute you're shooting mental daggers at me, the next you're oozing honey."

"I think it's a peculiarity we both share, Mr. Matthews."

Logan nodded, his smile suddenly fading as he appeared overcome by a paralyzing thought. "Wine!" he shouted dramatically. "I forgot the wine!"

"Don't fret so," Jill teased. "There's a bottle in the fridge. I bought it in town the other day."

"Ah," Logan answered as he opened the refrigerator to inspect her selection, "don't tell me you indulge in a nip once in a while. It's quite out of character. I thought you'd scream in vegetarian horror when I brandished those steaks!"

"They smell delicious."

"They'd better!" said Logan as he stabbed the browning meat with a fork.

Dinner was as luscious as Logan had predicted; Jill's appetite returned with each bite of the succulent meat.

"Tell me, Jill," Logan inquired as he cleared the table, pouring Jill another glassful of wine, "how do you rate my cooking?"

"Well," Jill smiled in response, "the salad was heavenly, but you have to confess that anyone could have produced the same results with the steaks . . . it's no major feat. So, taking that into consideration, I'll give you an eight on a scale of ten."

Doing his best to look wounded, Logan sat two bowls on the table. "We almost forgot the crowning glory . . . dessert!"

Suppressing a smile, Jill forced her face to remain stern.

Logan watched as Jill took a bite of the chocolate chip ice cream he had scooped out for her, patiently awaiting her critique.

"If it was cherry vanilla, you'd have yourself a ten. But since it isn't, the best I can do for you is a nine."

"How about if I do up the dishes and sweep up the floors?"

"Oh, Mr. Matthews," Jill taunted, "you mean you'd actually humble yourself to do woman's work?"

"I don't see why not," Logan answered, making a grand play out of retrieving one of Aggie's frilly aprons from a peg on the wall and tying it about his waist. "There's only one thing I want you to know."

"And what is that?" Jill asked on cue.

Stiffening his back, his face devoid of mirth, Logan divulged, "I don't do windows!"

Jill found herself assigned to the role of spectator as Logan held true to his promise. She sipped her wine, content to remain quiet while he clattered about quite efficiently. About to empty her glass with one last swallow, Jill looked up as Logan reached out and grasped her by the wrist, giving it a gentle press.

"Hold on a minute. I'd like to share a toast with you."

Watching as Logan filled his empty glass, Jill shook her head in refusal as he sought to replenish hers. Holding his glass out to the middle of the table, he waited for Jill to join him in the ceremony.

"I'd like to make a toast to a new start between us. Let's say that tonight is the first time we've met."

Mesmerized by the indefinable look on Logan's face, Jill clinked her glass against his. This was the Logan Matthews that Aggie evidently knew. He seemed in total contrast to the image Jill had garnered of him. She knew she was being seduced, and she found herself suddenly hungry for his attentions.

"Don't tell me I interrupted your reading again."

Jill followed the direction of Logan's gaze to the book she had carried with her just before his arrival, the small bound book of poems.

Not waiting for Jill's response, Logan strode to the chair and began thumbing through the pages.

"My," he said finally, "this stuff is pretty dreary."

"It depends on how you look at it," Jill answered defensively.

"I suppose you're right. I was never one for poetry, although some say I should be able to relate to a writer's drive. We're both the same when you come right down to it. When we create, we're totally alone with our inspiration. There's no way to share what comes from within . . . only a piece of paper and a slab of canvas can be party to the act."

Depositing himself with a thud into Aggie's kitchen rocker, Logan fixed a somber glance in Jill's direction.

"Now, tell me. Just who is Jill Barton?"

"I could very easily ask you the same question," Jill answered coolly.

"Ah." Logan laughed, shaking his finger at her in a scolding manner. "But I asked you first!"

"There's really nothing to tell," Jill said as she got up and started to pace the room.

"You want to remain a woman of mystery."

"It's not that. I just don't think dinner entitles you to be presented with my life as though it's one of my books you can thumb through and discard with a disparaging comment."

"I wouldn't do that, Jill."

Startled by the intimacy Logan's voice suggested, Jill gave herself leave to examine his motives more clearly. She stared at him, his eyes fixed on her in an unwavering dare.

Before Jill could speak, a resounding knock at the door jolted them both from the moment they had shared. Jill gasped in shock as the door opened without further hesitation. Filling the doorway stood Stacey Phillips.

"I saw a light in here, Logan. Whatever are you doing in the kitchen?"

Realizing Stacey hadn't even registered the fact that she was sitting in the chair, Jill took a step forward in preparation to leaving.

"You've hidden out long enough, Logan. We have to talk, and I'd like to do it now." Stacey's voice was kitten soft, her tone urging, pleading. She stepped forward, shyly reaching out for Logan, her hand touching his chest just above his heart. Logan's fingers closed over Stacey's, holding her hand there, and he moved a step closer to her.

Jill felt her heart wrench at the hungry expression in Logan's eyes as he looked down at the voluptuous woman with the sexy name. Neither of them seemed to notice when she slipped her arms into the sleeves of her heavy sweater. They ignored her as she called Doozey softly and then left the comfort and light of Logan's homey kitchen.

Seething with frustration that she recognized as illogical jealousy, Jill jogged down the road with Doozey at her heels. Running was supposed to take all the starch out of a person. It was working — she was exhausted.

Slowly, she walked back to her cabin. She made careful note to let her eyes stare at Briar Cottage. It was dark. Logan's house from the front was also dark, but the light was on in the upstairs bedroom area.

Six

"Ah, if it isn't our little writer!"

Jill turned in time to see Stacey Phillips, with a large lavender bath sheet over her arm. She nodded curtly and waited.

"I was just going to clean the bathroom," Jill volunteered quietly. Withdrawing the bucket and mop from the closet, she ignored the beautiful, if petulant, Stacey.

"In that case I'll wait. I hate to use a dirty bathroom."

"I'd hardly call this a dirty bathroom," Jill said tartly.

"Well, I would. Look, there're long black hairs in the bathtub," Stacey said, pointing a three-inch bloodred nail in the general direction of the sparkling tub.

Jill grimaced. "Are you going to stand there or what?" she demanded. "By the way, exactly what is your chore around here?"

"Chore?" Stacey said haughtily. "Sweetie, I am a guest. I don't do chores."

"But you've been eating here and using all

the facilities. You should do your share like everyone else," Jill said irritably.

Who did she think she was anyway? She grimaced again. She was Logan Matthews' lady friend, and possibly much more. Her own question and answer stung her to the quick. Jill grew more annoyed by the minute as she scoured out the tub and then ran clean water down the drain to wash away the residue left by the abrasive powder.

"You'll have to back out so I can mop the floor, Miss Phillips."

Stacey backed out, holding her luscious apricot dressing gown above her ankles.

"I do hate that pine smell. Do you have any Chanel you can spray around to cover the odor?"

Jill clenched her teeth. "I'm afraid not," she said politely. "If you wait another ten minutes the floor will be dry."

"Darling?"

Jill turned. "Yes?"

"How long are you planning on being here?"

"At least another week or until Aggie gets back," Jill said shortly.

"Then you'll still be here for Logan's going-away party, won't you?"

"Party?" Logan was going away. "Where is Mr. Matthews going?"

"Why, to Paris with me. Silly girl, didn't you know? Didn't someone tell you all about it? Usually you commune people spread rumors like wildfire."

Jill mumbled something unintelligible and left the room, her eyes blinded with salty tears. He really was going away. Now what was she going to do?

Suddenly, she was no longer hungry. Even Aggie's delicious homemade waffles couldn't tempt her this morning. She would go for a walk, timing her return for the end of the breakfast hour so she could help Aggie clean up.

How unfair life was, she thought morosely as she trudged down the sandy strip of beach. First, she was jilted at the altar. Then she was rejected before she even got to first base. Life was unfair. Why did girls like her always finish last? Why did the superelegant creatures like Stacey Phillips always walk off with the prize? For a while she had actually deluded herself into thinking that Logan might — and it was a big might — be just a little interested in her. He had kissed her as though he meant it. Surely, he had enjoyed those few intimate moments as much as she had.

Jill flopped down on the sand and stared out across the water. She forgot everything and let the waves hypnotize her. She lost all track of time and was only shaken from her thoughts by Doozey's loud barking. She turned and waved to the Irish setter. Doozey advanced, barked and then retreated. He repeated his frantic actions three more times till Jill got his canine message.

"Oh, you want me to come with you. Okay, Doozey, I'm coming."

She glanced at her watch. She still had time till breakfast was officially over. No sense in giving Logan Matthews cause for concern. She was doing her share, for that matter, more than she bargained for.

Doozey appeared to be upset. First he would bark, then growl and start to run. Every few feet he turned to see if she was still behind him.

"Don't tell me they forgot to feed you again," Jill mumbled as she skirted a sweeping jew at the beginning of the compound.

Startled by her close encounter with the spreading evergreen, Jill didn't see Logan Matthews until she collided with him.

"Oh, I'm sorry. It's my fault. I wasn't watching where I was going. I'm sorry."

"Come with me" was all Logan said.

Jill stared after the tall form. Now what? She hadn't done anything. She stood her ground.

"Where? Why?" she asked loudly.

Logan turned, his face cold and hard. "Because I said so."

Jill shrugged. He was calling the shots, or so it would seem. He was back to being his arrogant, obnoxious self. Puzzled at his attitude, she trotted along behind his long stride, Doozey in her wake, whining pitifully. Evidently, he didn't like his master's attitude either.

They stopped at the sanitation building. Logan held the door open for her and marched into the side that said Hers. Jill followed, more puzzled than ever. The sight that met her gaze stunned her. No wonder he was angry. Talcum powder was everywhere. Toothpaste oozed down the side of the sink and all around the faucets. A greasy, scummy oil with particles of hair from someone's razor lined the tub. The floor was saturated with water and dirty footprints. Jill gulped.

Logan crossed his hands over his chest. Jill had never seen such cold, dead eyes in her life. He said nothing, but waited.

"I cleaned it, truly I did. Then I went for a walk."

Logan's eyes clearly challenged her.

"You don't believe me, do you? Well, I don't care. I cleaned it, and when I left it was sparkling clean. Take a look at the other side, the side you men use. It's clean. When I left here your . . . your Miss Phillips was waiting to take her bath. She was here all the while I cleaned. She waited because she said she refused to bathe in a dirty bathroom. Even before I cleaned it, it didn't look like this. Don't ever, Mr. Matthews, call me a liar again."

Jill turned and ran as fast as she could back to Wynde Cottage. It wasn't until she was inside that she remembered she had to go to the dining hall to help Aggie. She couldn't even run away and pretend she had a class act. Now she had to go back and risk facing the artist and his steely eyes.

Waving to Aggie, Jill began clearing the table, careful to avoid Logan's eyes. He and Stacey had their heads together talking in low voices. Stacey's hands touched Logan again and again, picking imaginary lint from his sweater and smoothing his collar. Together, they made a cozy twosome.

Struggling with the cumbersome utility cart, Jill hunched over and started to push it across the dining hall. Her eyes were downcast to be certain the wheels didn't settle into the grooves in the plank floor. Before she knew what was happening, Logan had shouldered her aside and was pushing the cart into the back room where Aggie waited.

"I can do it. I've been doing it all week. If this is the way you apologize, you can just forget it, Logan," Jill hissed.

"It is an apology. I was hoping you would notice." His eyes twinkled and he reached out his hand. "Friends?"

How could she stay angry with him? Her heart soared, and then she remembered the lone light in the upstairs of Logan's house and the darkness at Briar Cottage. What had she expected? He did say *friends.* She nodded curtly and turned her back on him.

"A mite hard on him, weren't you?" Aggie said quietly.

"You didn't hear the way he talked to me, Aggie. He might just as well have called me a liar," Jill said defensively.

Aggie stopped what she was doing and stared at Jill.

"Logan is different from most men, Jill. He's caught up in his painting world. His eye only sees what it sees. What I'm trying to say is when he made his morning check his eyes saw a dirty bathroom. In all fairness to Logan, you cleaned up a half hour early today. Be fair."

"Okay, you've made your point, Aggie," Jill said, slightly mollified.

"What do you have planned for today? Anything special?"

"I thought I might write a little," she fibbed.

Aggie's eyes danced and her chins wobbled with mirth. "How is your book coming?"

"It's coming, but that's about it," Jill hedged.

"Do you think you'll be finished around four this afternoon?"

"Probably," Jill continued to hedge. "Why?"

"I thought if you weren't doing anything you could go with me to the show tonight. Cocktails and everything."

"What show? Cocktails where?"

"Gracious sakes, I forgot you didn't know. Miss Phillips arranged a showing in town this evening for Logan. He kicked up his heels, but Miss Phillips was adamant. Seems there's to be a lot of art critics coming at her special invitation. Mine is engraved. If you stop by the kitchen later, I'll show it to you. Think about it. Why don't you run along now and work on your book for a while? It will get your mind off this morning."

"Are you sure this isn't too much for you?" Jill asked, looking around.

"Good heavens, no. All I have to do now is wipe off the tables and I'm finished."

"If you say so," Jill said dubiously.

Now she was stuck with her lie. She would have to hide out at Wynde Cottage for a couple of hours and pretend she was working. There would be no walk for her this morning.

Straightening up the tiny cottage and making the bed took all of fifteen minutes. What was she to do with the rest of her time?

If she was careful she might make it to her car and take a ride around the countryside. This way she would be out of sight of the artists' colony and able to explore a bit at the same time. Aggie would never notice if she stayed in back of Logan's house, and Logan himself would probably be down at the beach painting. If Stacey noticed her leave, she could always say she wanted to make penciled notes or something equally stupid.

Jill roamed the countryside for several hours but did not appreciate the beauty of Rhode Island. How sad, she mused, that she couldn't relate in any way to the beauty surrounding her. She might as well go back. The car ate up the miles on the backcountry road more quickly than she would have liked. Driving through the gates of Mill

Valley, Jill had to inch her car over to the side of the road, almost going into a ditch. A battered Mustang, with its hood standing sentinel, was almost blocking the road. Jill pulled her car over and climbed out. She recognized the writer and grinned.

"What's wrong?"

"Beats me." Pat grinned back. "It just died on me. I can write about it, but I can't tell you what makes it tick. You don't by any chance know anything about engines, do you?" she asked hopefully.

"A little. Let me take a look," Jill said, grabbing her emergency tool kit from the luggage compartment.

For the next hour and a half Jill lost herself to the inner workings of the internal-combustion engine. She emerged with a grin stretching from ear to ear. The journalist laughed.

"You look awful. You have grease in your hair and all over your face."

"That's okay. I really enjoyed tinkering with your car. I must say it was a definite challenge. Let's see if it works. Start the engine. I want to see how it goes."

She was spared further comment when the baby-blue Porsche skidded to a stop. The horn blared, stopped, and then blared again. Jill walked away from the car and stood in the center of the road, her face a mask of dislike.

"You'll have to wait a minute until we see if it works."

The journalist turned the key and the sweet hum of a contented engine filled the quiet afternoon. Jill laughed delightedly.

"You really need a good overhaul," she said, slamming down the hood of the decrepit car.

"You must be one of the seven wonders of the world. Did you see and hear that engine?" the writer called out to the occupant of the Porsche. The door swung open and Logan Matthews stood towering over the small sports car.

His steely eyes were doing strange things, or was it the light coming through the maple trees? Jill was aware of how she must look and suddenly she didn't care.

"You said everything here was free." She laughed. "I'm just doing my thing."

She laughed again and the writer joined in as her engine turned over. Jill watched as the old car purred through the gates and out to the main road.

"Well, you can just do your thing somewhere else. You've held us up long enough. Your car is blocking half the road, or can't you see? That car, or pile of junk, should have been compacted ten years ago," Stacey Phillips shouted angrily.

Jill smirked; she couldn't help it. She always felt good when she made something work.

"If you can't maneuver that submarine out of here, I can do it for you." She giggled. "I didn't learn to drive via Sears Roebuck. Be my guest," Jill shouted as she bowed low with a wide sweeping of her arms.

Logan Matthews threw back his head and roared with laughter.

"Well done, Miss Barton. Well done. I, for one, applaud you. Perhaps you would be kind enough to take a look at my engine tomorrow. That is, if your book isn't going to occupy all of your time."

Jill giggled again. "Mr. Matthews, I would be delighted to look at your engine, your etchings, or whatever you want me to look at."

She waved and the Porsche burned rubber as it sped through the gates. Jill alternated between fits of laughter and giggles all the way back to Wynde Cottage. She gathered her towel, soap and bath oil together, along with a stack of clean clothes. She was back at the cottage an hour later with a book in her hand when Aggie walked through the door.

"I thought you were going to stop by?" she accused.

"I was, but I got sidetracked. That little journalist had some car trouble and I helped her fix it. Then I took a shower and lost track of time. By the way, what time is it anyway?"

"Almost time to leave for Logan's show. Are you ready?"

"Aggie, I can't go. I wasn't invited."

A vision of Stacey Phillips greeting her at the door and then pushing her back outside swam before her eyes.

"Of course you're going, Jill. If you don't go, I won't. And nothing is going to make me miss out on Logan's showing."

Aggie stood in the middle of Jill's sitting room, her face purple from frustration as she shook an engraved invitation at Jill.

"It says that I and a guest of my choice are invited to attend the gallery showing of Logan Matthews' seascapes. So don't say another word about it, Jill. You're the guest of my choice!"

Twirling in front of the bathroom mirror, Jill knew without a doubt that she had achieved perfection. Adjusting the tortoise-shell combs she had used to pull her hair back from her face, she watched as her reflection smiled back at her. It had taken her only a minute to select the mulberry jump-suit from the depths of the suitcase. Jill's eye had been caught by the creation the first moment she had seen it. The material was a type she had never seen before, giving the appearance of velour, yet lighter in weight. The shoulders capped the top of her arms and the neckline plunged to a simple knotted belt at the waist. As accessories, Jill had chosen a gold-banded bracelet and a pair of tiny gold earrings. To complete the style, she slid her feet into a pair of elegant gilt slippers. Necessity demanded that she wear a lightweight coat, and luckily, she just happened to have a stylish raincoat in the back seat.

Jill was rewarded with an exclamation of approval as Aggie opened her door.

"My, my! You're going to be the belle of the ball in that outfit!"

Giggling at the woman's playfulness, Jill felt the mounting excitement begin to churn in her stomach as they drove into Mill Valley. For some reason, Jill had pictured their destination as an imposing art gallery located somewhere in the middle of town. What she was greeted with was a rather os-tentatious building that appeared to be someone's home. The outside of the house reminded Jill of the gothic romances she used to read as a teenager. The architecture even boasted a turret room, and Jill looked up at the dimly lit windows, half expecting to see Jane Eyre staring down at her. It was soon evident in which direction they should head, for the sound of scores of voices drifted across the lawn from a set of opened French doors.

"Sounds like Stacey has gotten the whole town to show up!" Aggie remarked cheerfully.

Following Aggie's lead, Jill was unprepared for the pressing crush of people. Everyone seemed to be milling about aimlessly; only a selected group of guests were examining the array of artwork that had been cleverly arranged against one wall. Looking around for Logan, Jill nudged Aggie as she saw Stacey Phillips bearing down on them, her face struggling against a sneer.

"Mrs. Beaumont," she cooed as she relieved Jill and her companion of their wraps, "I'm so glad you were able to join us. Logan has already sold three of his paintings, and a second dealer from Paris is trying to convince him to accept a contract for a showing at his gallery!"

"You sound surprised, Miss Phillips,"

Aggie said as she twisted her hand out of the woman's grasp. "I knew all along that Logan would be a success."

"Yes," Stacey said contritely, eyeing Jill for the first time. "And who do we have here?"

"You've met Jill before, Miss Phillips. She's the young writer who's been staying in Wynde Cottage."

"That's right," Stacey answered, her eyes narrowing into catlike slits. "I just suppose I'm used to seeing you in those faded blue jeans while you scrub toilets."

Disregarding Stacey's barb, Jill pretended to see someone she knew and headed for a corner of the room where she could search the crowd for a glimpse of Logan. Aggie trailed after her, only to be grabbed by the arm and asked to assess Logan's latest work by a short little man in wire glasses. Jill laughed as the woman reeled off praise after praise, her body quivering with enthusiasm as she realized that she had latched on to an eager listener.

Out of the corner of her eye, Jill saw Logan come into the room from what looked to be an adjoining study. A tall man stood beside him, and as they shook hands and parted company Logan's face flashed a charming smile. Undoubtedly, he had just closed the deal with the man from Paris.

"There he is, Arlene! That's Logan Matthews!"

Startled from her clandestine observation, Jill accepted a glass of champagne from a waiter who was roaming the crowd. Two girls were seated on a small divan, their attention riveted on Logan.

"I'm telling you, Arlene," one of them whispered, pulling her friend closer as she noticed Jill standing nearby, "he's the most gorgeous man I've ever seen!"

The other girl snorted, obviously not convinced. "So what if he is? Not one woman in this room would have a chance with him. Stacey Phillips has her claws in him, and she's not one to let go."

"I suppose you're right," the girl finally relented. "She does hang over him, and he, evidently, doesn't mind. Still, it's a shame . . . a shame and a waste."

Jill sipped the champagne in a vain effort to dull the agony she felt as she looked across the room and saw Stacey slip her arm through Logan's. She should never have let Aggie talk her into coming. Logan was so absorbed in accepting praises that he didn't even know she was there. Even Aggie had sought out a comfortable chair, her head nodding in an unmistakable doze.

Jill walked around the small, crowded gallery, looking at one angry seascape after another. She was stunned when she came upon a small canvas, exquisitely framed in gold, of a calm sea. She stood back to admire the brush strokes. How unlike Logan this painting was; the giant frothy swells were absent and in their place was an expanse of placid water stained with the colors of sunset and the sky a dusky sapphire blue. The brush strokes were lighter, more delicate, the shading more subdued. Yet off in the distance could be seen an approaching storm, threatening the calm in the foreground. How strange she hadn't noticed it before. It was a painting of that particular spot on the beach where she had first seen Logan.

Jill moved on to the next painting. Again it was spectacularly framed. There was something disconcerting about it. The painting was a continuation of the calm sea, but the shading was darker, the brush strokes heavy and predominant, and the sea was a roiling brew of tumultuous surf. Spindrift dotted the canvas, and Jill could almost feel it spraying her cheeks, she could almost smell the tangy kelp depicted in the foreground and hear the salt sea crashing against the ominously black rocks. Andrew Wyeth, move over, you've just met your match, she muttered beneath her breath.

Stacey Phillips narrowed her eyes as she watched Jill gasp when she came upon the second of the paintings. A soft hiss escaped her lips. Deftly, she captured two cocktails from a passing waiter. "It's breathtaking, isn't it?" she said to Jill as she offered the champagne glass.

"Yes, it is," Jill agreed softly as she accepted the drink.

"Things seem to be under control here," Stacey told her. "Why don't we go out to the veranda and get away from some of this smoke? The noise and chatter is a bit much. Besides, I think it's time you and I became better acquainted."

It *was* stuffy in the gallery and a breath of air would feel good, Jill thought as she followed Stacey through the wide French doors. She felt uneasy about talking with Stacey, but she squared her shoulders and told herself that she could hold up her end of the conversation — unless, of course, it concerned Logan, and then she might have a problem. Safe topics of conversation would be called for.

Stacey set her drink down on a wrought-iron table and then leaned her elbows on the railing of the veranda. "Autumn is my favorite time of year. I first met Logan several years ago around this time. I'm very fond of him. I guess you know that, don't you?" She swung around suddenly, startling Jill.

Jill searched for the correct response. She had the distinct feeling she wasn't going to like the turn this conversation was going to take. "I . . . I think that most people who know Logan are fond of him. I haven't known him that long but I like him. . . ."

"Yes, I know. Too much, it would seem. That's why I wanted to have this little talk. I suspect you have some sort of infatuation for him, and my suspicions were confirmed when I saw your reaction to his paintings. More than just a passing interest, wouldn't you say? Is it possible you're in love with him?" Stacey asked softly, her eyes glitteringly hard in the dim light.

Jill swallowed hard. The question was so soft, barely a whisper, that she felt she must have misunderstood. But the calculating look in Stacey's eyes told her she had heard right the first time.

"I don't think what I feel or don't feel for Logan is important, and it certainly isn't something I want to discuss in idle cocktail chatter," Jill answered coolly.

"You're right. It isn't important to me, but it could be to you. If you do love Logan, that is. You see, my dear, I'm going to marry Logan in Paris. Look," she said, opening the slim purse she had set down beside her glass and withdrawing an envelope. "Two plane tickets to Paris. One for Logan and one for me. Now you see why it's important for you not to be infatuated with him. Nothing can come of it. Logan belongs to me. He always has. Oh, I grant you I gave him a bit of a hard time last year when I thought . . . never mind. That's not important either. Fortunately, for Logan and myself, I came to my senses in time. We were meant for each other. We have so much in common. His work, my gallery, the whole art world for that matter. You don't fit in, darling. It's as simple as that. In more plain terms, you're out of your league, little girl."

Jill felt as though the breath had been driven from her body with a resounding blow. It couldn't be! Stacey must be lying. Logan asked her to marry him! Logan and Stacey! Yet she had seen the plane tickets. And she couldn't believe Stacey would lie about something so important. Jill groped for words. She had to say something, anything, to get away from the smiling woman with the narrowed eyes. Stacey was enjoying herself at Jill's expense. "Congratulations," she managed quietly. Get away from here, her mind shrieked, get away from here, go somewhere quiet where you can be alone.

You can't let her see how this has stunned you. That's what she wants. "I think it's time for me to leave now." Amazing. Did that calm voice really belong to her?

"Darling. I've upset you. That wasn't my intention," Stacey cooed. "It was just that I could see the direction you were heading, and I don't want to see you hurt. He's like the sea he paints. Parts of him are channeled and controlled and then he's whipped into a powerful and masterful force. I call him angry god of the sea."

Jill was furious. The last statement was uncalled for; there was no need to rub salt in the wound. Her own eyes narrowed as she turned to face Stacey. "I'm certain you and Logan will be very happy and I wish you well. Now, if you'll excuse me, I think it's time I was getting back to the compound."

"That would probably be best," Stacey said, following Jill back inside the crowded room. "I enjoyed our little talk. I find it pays to get things out into the open. This way there's no room for misunderstanding."

"You're absolutely right." Without another word Jill weaved her way through the crowd and down the steps to the small parking lot. She had to be alone, if even for a moment, before she went back for Aggie.

Logan was going to marry Stacey Phillips.

Logan was going to . . . Over and over the words ricocheted through her brain. How could she have been so blind? How could she have thought she had a chance with him?

It was time to leave Mill Valley. Time to go back where she belonged. The question was, should she leave before Logan and Stacey left for Paris or should she leave immediately? Tomorrow was another day, she thought wearily. She would make her decision in the bright light of day, not in the dark that was as confused as her jumbled thoughts.

Jill squeezed her eyes shut against the darkness in her cottage, trying desperately to welcome sleep. Her body ached, crying out in loud refusal to her efforts to relax. The ride back to Mill Valley had been a quiet one, punctuated only by Aggie's snoring, confirming Jill's decision to take the wheel. She had been thankful the woman had napped soundly beside her, for she knew her weak rein on her tears would be broken if Aggie had asked her about her evening.

Damn Logan Matthews! Her hasty retreat from the showing had been the only thing that had caught his observance. Jill had helped Aggie into her coat only to look up and see Logan advancing on them through the crowd. He had looked so triumphant, so happy. How could he be so hypocritical? Why did she feel so betrayed?

The roar of an engine whizzed past Jill's cottage, pulling her from the bed to investigate. Even before she parted the curtains, she knew what she would see. Stacey's Porsche had come to a halt in front of Logan's house. Jill turned her back on the scene, certain she had spared herself the torture of seeing them both get out of the car and walk inside.

Unable to stand it, Jill jumped back into bed, pulling the covers over her head, needing to hide from the hurt of losing something she had never really had.

Seven

The dim gray light of dawn pierced through the curtains of Jill's window and found her still awake. The sheets were twisted around her legs. The pillows had suffered the torture of weary poundings and the coverlets had spilled onto the floor. Sleep had been impossible; thoughts of Logan and Stacey Phillips' cooing voice had haunted her. Whatever she had hoped for, whatever she had dreamed, had come to an end.

Throwing her legs over the side of the bed, Jill walked around the cottage, pulling on her jeans and a sweater. Glancing back at the bed, she frowned, "The princess and the pea," she muttered, kicking the covers out of her way. "Only I'll bet my last two bucks it wasn't a pea that kept her awake. It must have been a man!"

In the shadowy darkness of daybreak, she stumbled into her sandals, knowing her feet were going to be frozen. If she couldn't sleep, then she would walk. Walk and walk. Walk from here to Timbuktu, wherever that was, if she had to. She only knew she couldn't bear another minute of cloistering herself in this cottage.

When she opened the door, the slightest of breezes that accompanies dawn pushed billows of fog into the room. It was a low fog, reaching out and embracing the earth, swirling around her knees and making her sandaled feet damp and cold. Impervious to the discomfort, she placed one foot in front of the other and marched toward the beach.

The sound of the breakers came to her before she could see them. The rising sun had not dissipated the fog, although there were indications that it would burn off later in the day. Jill's long golden hair was loose, and now it was damp, almost wet. The thick, heavy sweater was sticking to her uncomfortably, but it was too chilly to remove it. These early-morning hours were as miserable as she felt.

Leaving the road, her foot touched sand. The sound of the surf was closer, but all she could see ahead was vast grayness. The same vague grayness her own future held — a future without Logan Matthews.

Down at the water's edge the hypnotic flowing and ebbing of the tide waves held her mesmerized. The sky was becoming lighter now as her thoughts became darker, ebbing into night and beyond. *Desolate, alone* — words that could frighten her dominated her thoughts. *Lost, forgotten* — words that damned were the curse of her destiny.

Her arms wrapped around her, and she hunched her shoulders, seeking warmth, pleading easement from this abandonment. The tears ran down her cheeks, blending with the salt spray as she turned her steps to the beach, to the far outcrop of rocks from which she had watched Logan that first day, eternities ago.

Inwardly, she scolded herself, berating her foolishness. A midnight visit to her cottage and unexplored passions did not make a relationship. There were no commitments, no vows, no words of love. There was nothing and there would be nothing. She had managed to pull herself up by her bootstraps once when she was jilted by Deke, and she would again. Although somehow the end of the relationship with Deke hadn't wounded her the way the thought of Logan belonging to someone else did.

Prophetically, a thin golden shaft of sunlight pierced the wispy fog. It was possible now to discern the far horizon. Throwing back her shoulders and lifting her chin, Jill walked along the shore, her feet keeping time to a rhythmic drumming in her head.

It was then that she saw him, leaning against the rocks, looking off into the distance. His Irish woolen sweater enhanced his broad shoulders and defined his tapered waist. His long, denim-clad legs supported him in an easy balance. The wind had played through his night-dark hair, rippling it into stray curls and waves that fell over his brow and tumbled roguishly over his ears. Suddenly, as though sensing her presence, he turned and saw her.

Jill turned on her heels, gulping air, knowing only that she must get away from him, leave him. Otherwise she could never rebuild her life. Desperation lengthened her stride; rejection quickened her pace; hopelessness pounded in her breast.

"Jill!" Her name carried across the sand, losing itself in the fog. The sound of his voice held a command, an order that she halt.

She ran, her breath coming faster, her heart pounding louder. The loose sand rolled beneath her feet, slowing her pace. The light wind lifted her hair, pulling it back from her face, exposing it to the misty vapor surrounding her.

She knew he was close behind her. She imagined she could hear the deep breaths he was taking, and then she heard him call her name once again. "Jill!"

Gone was the command, the order. In its place was a plea, a hope. Still, she ran. There was no hope, no survival if she stayed. Jill ran, ran for her life.

"Jill!"

His voice was closer now, stronger, coming to her through the air, blown to her on the breeze. Her steps faltered; she struggled to keep balance, determined to keep running.

His hand came from behind her, staggering her, spinning her around. "Let go of me!" She struggled desperately, fighting.

He was trying to say something, tell her something, but the panic was erasing all her senses, everything except the need to run. She kicked at his shins with her sandaled feet, twisting to escape like some trapped feline.

The edge of hysteria was evident in her voice. As if he sensed it, he seized her shoulders and shook her violently until she thought her neck would snap.

"Let me go!" she demanded again when he had stopped shaking her. She still struggled to free herself of him.

His hold tightened, biting into her flesh beneath the thick sweater, refusing to set her free, holding her firm.

"I hate you! I hate you! Let me go!"

His eyes blazed down at her, singeing her with their fury. His mouth tightened grimly, a mask of rage. A muscle convulsed in his jaw, giving proof of his furor. Before she could protest further, he captured her hands and held her arms behind her back, and she was crushed against him, trapped, imprisoned, cornered.

The salty scent of the ocean was in his sweater, but beneath it was the male scent of him, heady and potent. Her senses were sharp, alert, watchful. Driven by her desperation to escape, she struggled again, writhing against him, her pulses pounding.

The broadness of his shoulders became her pummeling posts, as she beat against him, bending backward, forcing him to follow.

Together, they dropped to the sand, tumbling over and over, grappling for supremacy. Logan's power intensified, the sheer brawn of him making her conflict strenuous and labored. Choking tears tore her throat, heaving sobs stifled her breath. Wordlessly, he gripped both sides of her head, forcing her to be still, freezing her into immobility. She was helpless, conquered, and cold fear stabbed her when she at last lifted her eyes to his.

The bruising possession of his mouth was

an assault. His anger stiffened his body against hers, holding her firm, denying her escape. Her cold fear was replaced by his fire, licking up and down her spine. Still she fought, as though for her very life. Stronger now, fortified by obstinacy, she used her arms to wedge a space between them, frustrating his efforts to crush her again in his unyielding arms.

His hands circled her throat, forcing her chin up, making her mouth vulnerable to his. His lips held her captive, covering hers firmly, warmly. Stubbornly she tried to pull away, but he tightened his hold on her neck. His kiss deepened searchingly; hot flames touched her toes and flickered up her legs, centering somewhere in the center of her being.

Her small cries of surrender were conceived in her throat and born on her lips. His name began as a curse and became a prayer as he held her, pressed her into the sand, covering her with the length of him.

She was without will as his hands touched her. Her resolve became a vapor as his lips traveled the slim column of her neck, finding their reward in the throbbing pulse he found below her ear. When his hands cupped her breasts, a flaming desire ignited within her to know the fullness of his possession.

Her arms circled his neck, capturing him in her embrace. Her lips were her offering; her body was created to please him. Low sounds rumbled in his chest, heightening her awareness of him, delighting her senses.

The wings of trapped birds fluttered in her breast when resistance reasserted itself. His mouth opened over hers, parting her lips, tasting the sweetness he found there. The ocean roared in her head, pounding, eroding her will.

Logan lifted his head, looking down into her upturned face. He gazed at her for a moment, his eyes alive with a vibrant passion she had never seen in another man's eyes. Jill reached up to touch his face, caressing his jaw. He buried his face in her neck, his mouth stirring a twin desire in her. His caresses traveled the length of her, leaving her breathless, her heart nearly bursting as she exulted in his touch.

"Logan, Logan, I love you," she breathed, her murmurs a confession of the feelings she could deny no longer.

Logan's body stiffened, pulling away in abrupt denial, leaving her confused and abandoned. Pulling himself upright, he sat gazing out at the sea for a long moment. She lay still, watching him, seeing his turmoil in the wrinkling of his brow and the grim set of his mouth.

What had she done? Why had he pulled away from her? Was he still playing games? Awakening her one moment and rejecting her the next. She should hate him! Hate him with every fiber of her body. But somehow it was impossible to hate Logan Matthews. Every instinct told her he had been sincere each time he had pressed his lips to hers. She had felt it in his touch, in the urgency of his passion, in the tenderness of his lovemaking.

At last he turned to her, looking down at her, touching her hair with his fingertips.

"Jill, you're so young. I'm not certain you know what love is all about."

Logan's voice was soft, almost a whisper.

"I can learn, Logan," she heard herself say, but when she looked up it was to find him gone. He was walking down the beach, away from her.

Today was to be Aggie's last day before leaving for Seattle. She was "packed and rarin' to go," as she had put it to Jill. Today, she had said, was going to be like any other day until the dinner hour was over. Then and only then would she leave. Logan was taking her to the airport. In other words, it was business as usual, she had said succinctly.

Jill felt as though she had lead weights tied to her feet as she went about her chores. The sun had burned off the fog but she didn't want to face the day or Logan Matthews. Facing herself in the tiny bedroom mirror, her cheeks blotched with tears, was all the facing up she was going to do for a long time to come. She should leave, she told herself, but something was holding her back. Hope? Fool, she told herself. Men like Logan Matthews killed hope. They set about their orderly lives, and if you were included, you could count yourself lucky. If not, you could consider yourself hopeless.

A feeling of impending doom seemed to be settling over her. The feeling was so strong she shivered. What else could go wrong that would or could possibly matter to her? It wasn't that she was going to be in charge of the kitchen chores. Aggie had said that her new friend, Pat the journalist, and Jack were to be her new helpers. No, she could manage the chores. It was something else. She tried to shake the feeling, but it stayed with her while she cleaned the bathrooms, and it was still with her when she walked forlornly to the dining hall.

Doozey ran toward her just as she reached the front door.

"Hi ya, Doozey. How have you been? Haven't seen you for a while," Jill said, scratching the setter behind the ears.

"He's been punished for digging in the garbage," a voice said behind her.

Jill ignored Logan Matthews and walked into the dining hall. She walked as quickly as she could to the opposite side of the room and sat down. She couldn't face him, didn't want to face him, not after he had left her alone on the beach wearing her heart on her sleeve.

"Mind if I sit down?"

"And if I did, would you leave? It's your dining hall, Mr. Matthews, sit anywhere you please."

"Testy this morning, aren't we?"

"That's as good a word as any I could come up with," Jill snapped.

"I thought you would like the word. After all, words are your business. I'm just a lowly painter. You writers seem to have the world cornered as far as emotional words are concerned. By the way, how are your memoirs coming?"

Jill fidgeted. She hated it when he brought up the lie she had told him. She squirmed in her seat and shrugged. "I'm far from a professional" was all she could manage.

"It must be tedious work, trying to remember all the details of your life."

It sounded to Jill like a statement of fact that required no answer. She shrugged again, wishing the waiters would get on with serving breakfast. Where was Stacey Phillips? Now, that was a loaded question, and she would dearly love a loaded answer.

"What are you serving for my going-away party?"

"I wasn't aware that you were going away, much less having a party," Jill fibbed. "Nothing was said to me about having extra duties. I have my hands full as it is."

"It's not an order," Logan replied just as coolly. "What we usually do is have cake and coffee the night before one of the guests is due to leave. Very simple fare."

"Guess that lets me out, then. I can't bake," Jill said, watching the door carefully for some sign of Stacey.

Logan got to his feet and stood towering over her. Gone was his playfulness and humor. His eyes were narrowed to slits as he stared down at her. For a moment Jill remembered the odd feeling of impending doom she had experienced on awakening.

"By the way, a call came in for you this

morning, quite early, as a matter of fact. I took the message and left it on the desk in the office. Someone by the name of Deke called."

Jill swallowed hard. Impending doom was too tame a phrase. She felt all the color drain from her face. Unconsciously, she grasped the edge of the table, her knuckles white against the burnished maple.

"He sounded like an anxious husband to me," Logan said coldly. "I know I must be mistaken because you said you weren't married when you registered."

Jill was stunned. It was impossible! There was no way, absolutely no way, for Deke to find her. By rights, she should be as safe in Mill Valley as she was if she were on the moon. How had Deke found her? And, more important, what did he want? Wasn't he satisfied that he had left her standing at the altar? Wasn't her humiliation enough?

Jill felt numb as she stared at Logan, willing words to her tongue.

"I am not married."

That was all. There was nothing more to say. The steely eyes penetrated her being. The anger on his face that first day on the beach had been nothing compared to what she was seeing now.

Jill was silent a moment longer and then

turned and left the dining hall. Her voice had been cool, almost impersonal. Amazing. She was dying on the inside, and she could be as cool as the proverbial cucumber on the outside. Her shoulders slumped the moment she was outdoors. How could Deke have found her? Her mind raced frantically, trying to reconstruct an answer to the riddle. Unless someone had searched her belongings, there was no way that she could be connected to Deke Atkins. She hadn't mailed the postcards to Nancy and the girls.

Jill raced back to her cottage and looked in her handbag. All was as it should be. The postcards. She turned, expecting to see them on the dresser. No, that had been in Briar Cottage. Before Stacey took it over!

"Oh, no!" she wailed. Aggie, when she straightened the cottage for Stacey, or Stacey herself must have mailed them, thinking that was what Jill wanted.

Call Deke, she told herself. She turned in the direction of the door and then suddenly sat down on the bed. No. She didn't want to talk to him. She couldn't face that today. It would be an ugly scene because she felt ugly inside.

Pack and leave! her mind ordered. "I can't," she whispered. "If I leave now, I'll never see Logan again, and I don't want to remember him with that anger in his eyes. After the party."

A going-away party for Logan! How in the world was she going to handle that? Perhaps if he had just made some mention of his impending marriage to Stacey it would have cleared the air between them.

A party. Colorful party plates, balloons, streamers . . . all the trimmings. Was she expected to go all out for this bon voyage affair? Cake and coffee sounded simple enough. But a party wasn't really a party without the festive accoutrements, and with Aggie in Seattle this was more than she felt she could handle.

Somewhere in the laundry area she recalled seeing a box with a handmade label stating simply Party Decorations. Undoubtedly, Aggie had a varied assortment of trimmings. She promised she would check it out as soon as she checked the larder to be certain all the ingredients were on hand to bake the cake. It shouldn't be too difficult, not with Aggie's own handwritten recipes in the little tin box by the stove.

Jill determined this was not going to be a bland affair. She would outdo herself. No one, not ever, would know what this effort would cost her. If she was lucky, she might even be able to choke down some cake and swallow the coffee.

Facing Logan and pretending happiness for him would be so hard. Could she do it? Of course, she had no other choice. Stacey Phillips would get Logan, and she, Jill, would salvage her pride. A very poor comparison no matter how she looked at it. But a necessary one.

Selecting a recipe for Black Forest Cake, Jill rummaged in Aggie's cabinets till she found a suitable bowl for mixing a double batch of batter. The heavy ceramic bowl was cheerful, with a clever pattern of Indian design around the sides and trailing to the bottom of the bowl. For some reason it cheered Jill as she measured and then sifted the flour into the huge cavity.

Her preparations were well under way and the oven was heating when Jill was aware of a presence in the room. She stopped greasing the cake tins and looked around. It was quiet. Just the soft music coming from the radio perched on top of the refrigerator. She looked around again, an uneasy feeling creeping between her shoulders.

"Anyone there?" she called in the direction of the laundry room. There was no response. The strange feeling stayed with her until she slid the cake pans into the oven. She quickly set the small timer on the stove and just as quickly strode into the laundry room. It was empty. No sound at all came from the small area. Her eyes went to the screen door. Latched. She shrugged; it must be her imagination. She was on edge, there was no doubt about it. If she didn't watch it, she would get the heebie-jeebies, seeing and hearing strange noises that didn't exist. Actually, it wasn't anything that could be seen or heard. Only a dreadful feeling.

The alien feeling stayed with her while she sorted through the party box. Everything was there — paper plates with matching napkins; multicolored streamers and a fresh package of balloons. There was even an assortment of noisemakers. She would take them over to the dining hall as soon as the cakes came out of the oven. Just before the party, she would blow up the balloons and string them along the beams. Logan would appreciate the pains she had taken for his party. He might even thank her. But she didn't want thanks. She wanted Logan.

Jill shook her head. She had no right thinking such thoughts. Not now, since Stacey Phillips had confided their plans. She had to keep busy so she wouldn't think.

A glance through the glass window on the

oven door told her the cakes were rising evenly, so she set about washing up the utensils she had used. Next, she readied the fruit and mixed the frosting. When she was finished, she still felt jittery and out of control. The feeling of impending doom stayed with her while she made herself a cup of coffee, and it was still with her when she removed the cakes from the hot oven thirty minutes later.

While she sipped her coffee she mentally ran over the dinner menu in her mind. Spaghetti and meatballs. All she had to do was heat the frozen sauce and meat that Aggie had left in the freezer. The spaghetti would cook at the last minute, so her time for the most part was all right. She would even have time for a bath while the sauce heated and the water boiled. She grimaced as she wondered what she would do if she really were a writer. With all she had to do she would have had to forgo sleep in order to accomplish anything at all. Still, she wouldn't have missed this experience for anything. Meeting Aggie and having her for a friend was one good thing that had come of it.

If only things had worked out differently it would have been a memorable experience, one that would have lasted a lifetime, an experience that she and Logan could have shared together. Now he was going to share it with Stacey Phillips.

Jill straightened her shoulders. She couldn't think about this now, she warned herself, or soon the tears would start to flow and she would end up feeling sorry for herself all over again.

It was hard to tell from Logan's expression if he was pleased with the party decor or not. He seemed preoccupied, almost in another world. Stacey spoke to him several times before she could gain his attention. Jill watched, a puzzled expression on her face, as she sliced through the thick frosting, down through the layered fruit and fluffy cake until her knife touched the plate.

There were oohs and aahs as the guests stared at the mouthwatering dessert. Even Logan favored her with a smile. "I thought you said you couldn't bake," he teased lightly.

Jill's tongue felt thick, rendering her speechless. She could only stare at him for a moment before she handed him his plate and fork. Logan's eyes were dark and unreadable as he matched her gaze.

Stacey shouldered her way between the two chairs, literally pushing Jill from Logan's side. "Let me see this confectionery delight," she demanded. Then, more shrilly: "Darling, I couldn't possibly eat this. It would add twenty pounds immediately. For shame, Jill! Didn't you give any thought to us girls when you baked this cake?"

"Then don't eat it," Jill snapped as she headed back to the far end of the table, where she left the cake for quick disposal by the rest of the little group.

Forcing herself to take part in the festivities, Jill joined in a toast to Logan. "To good friends," Aaron said happily. "Here's hoping you have a safe and profitable journey, Logan." The others joined in as they attacked the rich dessert.

Jill was tasting the cake, her fork poised in midair, when the door to the dining hall opened and a voice called out, "Hello!"

Logan rose from the table and the others quieted, a hush falling over the room. A stranger in the compound at this hour of the evening was a rarity.

Jill froze as the man walked farther into the center of light. Deke!

"I'm looking for Jill. I'm Deke Atkins," he said, holding out his hand to Logan. The men shook hands briefly as Logan turned to look for Jill.

"There's someone here to see you, Jill. Sit

down, Mr. Atkins. Have a cup of coffee and a piece of cake."

Jill clenched her teeth as she made her way over to the table. The easy camaraderie was broken with Deke's arrival. The men finished their cake and Pat started to clear the table. Stacey remained quiet, her eyes narrowed and watchful. Neither Logan nor Stacey looked as though they were going to move or say anything.

"Deke" was all Jill could manage to say. Why had he come here? After his phone call to her she should have followed her instincts and called him back. Told him to stay away from her, that she never wanted to see him again. But she hadn't. She had run away from an unpleasant situation and buried her head in the sand, hoping it would go away. And now he was here, in the flesh, and what might have been unpleasant on the phone was going to be a face-to-face confrontation.

"I had a devil of a time finding you, Jill. Look, is there somewhere we could go and talk? I have a lot of things to tell you. I'm not interrupting anything, am I?" he asked, finally noticing the silence.

"Not at all, Atkins. It's just a small going-away party with a few friends. Jill was good enough to bake the cake and serve it. Sure there isn't anything we can get you after your long drive? Jill has a few things to do, and then she'll be right with you."

Why was Logan speaking for her as if she were a child? She could answer for herself. She steeled her resolve. Just because Deke had arrived on the spot didn't mean a thing. She could send him on his way with a few choice words, either in public or in private. She owed him nothing. She had burned her bridges when she left New Jersey.

"If you'll wait a few minutes, Deke, I'll be glad to listen to anything you have to say." Before I send you packing, she added under her breath. Busily, she stacked the dishes and set about clearing the table.

Jill worked feverishly tidying up the service area. Out of the corner of her eye she watched Logan and Stacey eye her with speculation. Deke toyed with a cup of coffee, saying nothing, not even bothering to try to make simple conversation. She placed the dish towel on the rack just as Deke stood up.

"Ready?" he called.

Jill nodded to Stacey and Logan and followed Deke outside into the crisp autumn night.

"You look well, Jill."

"I'm wonderful," she told him, realizing

with a sense of amazement that it was really true. She was wonderful. Regardless of her disappointment over Logan, she was wonderful. A sense of security in her own worth was something she had only recently found and would never relinquish. "Why are you here, Deke? What do you want? If memory serves me correctly, you left me standing at the altar. Offhand, I would say that finishes things between us. I simply cannot imagine why you're here now. You left me, remember? No phone call, nothing. You just didn't show up." Her voice was heated now, hard with anger. Not because she had been left standing at the altar but because he was here, trying to walk back into her life.

"Jill, I know what I did was unforgivable. I have no excuse. I got cold feet, it's as simple as that. I came here to see if just maybe you might find it in your heart to forgive me. I know I have no right to ask anything of you after what I did to you, but I had to try. All I can say is I'm sorry."

"I'm sorry too, Deke. It's too late."

"Can we at least be friends? After all, we're going to be working in the same office when you get back. I'd like to give it a try if you're willing. We really did have some good times together if you stop and think about it."

"I don't know, Deke, about us being friends. I don't think it would work. It's true that I'm going to be going back to the office, but only on a temporary basis. I plan to give my notice and then I'll wait until they replace me so I don't leave them shorthanded. I really don't think there's a future for either of us."

"There must be something left," Deke pleaded. "I expected you to be angry and throw me out on my ear. We're talking calmly like adults, so you can't be all that upset with me."

"I've had a lot of time to think since I got here, Deke. What happened was for the best. At first I was angry and humiliated, but I'm over that now. We all have to grow up sometime. Perhaps if you had been decent about it and called me to tell me you didn't want to marry me, things would be different. I'm not saying for sure that I would forgive and forget and take you back, but I might at least have some respect for you. It's over, Deke. By the way, when did you get here? Were you anywhere near the kitchen this afternoon? I had the feeling someone was watching me."

"Yes, it was me," Deke said glumly. "After I got here I sort of walked around for a while looking for you. I just wanted to see what you could be doing in a place like this. And I wanted to see if you were happy. I told myself if you were happy I would leave and go back to New York and not even bother letting you know I was here. But you looked so forlorn and miserable as I stood outside the window watching you. It took me a long time to get my nerve up to go over to the dining hall. I know you find this hard to believe, but I really do want to marry you. Jill, why couldn't you have waited instead of taking off the way you did? If you had been just a little patient, a little more understanding, we could be married and honeymooning in Hawaii. I knew by the next day that I had made a mistake, so it's just as much your fault as it is mine."

Jill grinned. "I *was* a jilted bride. You must be more of a fool than I thought if you think you can come here and expect to pick up where we left off — rather, where *you* left off."

"You must really hate me."

Jill's face grew serious. "No, Deke, I don't hate you. I even understand and I'm sorry that you made the trip up here for nothing. I'm leaving here in a little while myself. Why don't we say goodbye now and forget everything that's happened? You get on with your life and I'll get on with mine."

"I know that you're going to regret this someday, Jill. Someday you'll wish you hadn't been so hasty and foolish."

But Jill knew now that she was free, free of Deke by her own choice, free of Logan even, but not by her own choice.

"Goodbye, Deke," Jill said, holding out her hand.

Deke stared at Jill a moment and then lowered his eyes to her hand. Without a word he turned and walked toward his car.

While Jill threw her clothes into her bag she could hear Deke's engine cough and sputter. She grinned to herself. All the money he had paid for his sports car and he couldn't get it started. It would be just her luck to have to give him a ride, or worse yet, tow him to a garage. Her eyes widened. He wouldn't, he couldn't, be doing it on purpose. He could just sit there till it snowed before she would give him a lift anywhere.

"Doozey, come back here with my handbag!" Jill shouted as she closed the last of her cases. Where had the setter come from? He must have been sleeping under her bed all this time. "Doozey! Come back here. Doozey!" The setter ran across the compound, the contents of her purse spilling as he raced toward Stacey and Logan, who were talking to Deke.

By the time Jill reached the middle of the compound, Logan was bending over, gathering up the spilled contents. He spoke sternly to Doozey, who rolled over on his back to show he was sorry.

"I think that's all of it," Logan said, holding out the oversize purse. "My apologies. Doozey must have thought there was candy in your bag." She couldn't miss the strange coldness that permeated his voice.

Jill reached out to take her bag. "Thank you," she said quietly as she headed back to the cottage. One by one she carried her cases to the car and unceremoniously dumped them in the back seat. She turned the key and was rewarded with a low, throaty engine roar.

Suddenly, in her rearview mirror, she saw Deke's car come to life and his oversize wheels kick up dust as he zoomed out of the compound.

Sighing, Jill steered her car in his wake, only to stop quickly when Stacey's arms flew up, signaling. "What is it?" Jill asked, alarmed.

"Wait, you forgot something!" Stacey said sweetly. "I'll get it for you. I won't be a second."

As Stacey dashed off Logan turned to face Jill. "It would have been nice if you had told someone you were leaving. It is usual practice to give one's notice."

This was almost more than Jill could take. It would have been nice if he cared that she was leaving instead of only worrying about who was going to scrub the bathrooms. "Look, Mr. Matthews. I really don't owe you anything. Notice or otherwise. I worked my fingers to the bone around here. I did more than my share. That makes us even in my eyes. And I didn't know notice was required. I find that I have pressing business at home that I must attend to. I want to thank you for allowing me to stay here. Please say goodbye to the others for me, especially Aggie." In spite of herself, Jill found that her voice had softened and lost its edge.

"And would that pressing business happen to be Deke Atkins? You're not on his trail, are you?" There was a strange glint in Logan's eyes — anger, hostility, disappointment?

"Is that what you and Deke were talking about?" she asked. She wouldn't have put it past Deke to tell Logan an outright lie. Deke had pride; it would be too much for him to admit that he had driven all the way from New Jersey to be turned down by Jill.

Before Logan could answer, Stacey Phillips came down the path holding out a cloud of billowing white froth — Jill's wedding gown that she had discarded in the closet of the cottage that Stacey now occupied. "Darling, here. You certainly can't leave this behind. I know you'll be needing it."

All Jill could see were Logan's cold, chiseled features. In that one split second his eyes accused, judged and convicted. "You keep it. You'll need it long before I will," Jill said hoarsely.

Stacey's tinkling laugh followed her all the way to the gates. Logan's dark, unreadable eyes would haunt her for days to come. Would she ever be able to erase that memory of his face from her mind? He thought she had lied to him, lied to him all along. Tears pricked and stung her eyelids. She loved Logan and she could no more erase him from her mind or heart than she could stop breathing.

Jill drove down the highway and doubled back for the strip of beach where she had spent those few moments of unleashed passion with Logan. She knew it was a mistake to get out of the car to walk the sands at this time of night, but she felt a searing need to be near the water that Logan loved to paint. All she wanted was one last walk, one last look.

Jill kicked off her shoes and set them on

her car hood. The sand felt cool to her tired feet. She walked to the water's edge and tested it with her toe. It was as cold as the depths of Logan's eyes.

She walked back to one of the dunes and sat down. Intently, she stared out at the water, willing something to ease the ache in her heart. Several long quiet minutes were suddenly broken by Doozey, toppling her backward, licking her face.

"Doozey! What are you doing here? Of course I know you love to run the beach at night, but this is pretty far from home for you. You'd better get back before Logan starts to look for you."

Banishing Doozey to home, Jill went back to her car. Within a few minutes the highway was beneath her wheels. The window near her left shoulder was open and the crisp autumn air blew against her cheeks.

The white line on the road blurred in her vision. She was tired, too tired to drive all night long as had been her plan. Making a left at the turnoff that led into town, she changed her plans and decided to spend the night in the local motel. Besides, Aggie was returning home tomorrow morning and Stacey and Logan would be leaving. By early afternoon Aggie should be home and it would be safe to go back and say her goodbyes in person. Jill had come to love Aggie and could almost feel the older woman's strong, comforting arms around her.

Jill whispered Logan's name, the sound of it stolen away by the wind passing her window. She wouldn't cry; she had cried her tears for him. Now she was going to try to banish him from her soul. She made a silent resolution to convince herself that the man she dreamed of, the man she loved, had never really existed at all.

Eight

A low, angry wind raced around Logan's house as Jill knocked on the back door to see Aggie.

"I've seen some tired-looking people in my day, but you sure beat them all," Aggie Beaumont said as she held the kitchen door open for Jill. "You been crying too, I can tell," she added matter-of-factly. "Come on in. I'll make us both a cup of tea. Tea fixes everything," she said, a note of authority in her voice.

The minute Jill sat down at the table, she reached for Aggie, longing to feel those comforting arms around her. Bit by bit, fighting back tears, dry-eyed, she told Aggie her entire story. She left nothing out.

"I feel so helpless, Jill. I've known Logan all his life. Once that man makes up his mind the heavens themselves can't make him change it. I know that's not what you want to hear, but it's true. I think you were wrong to leave. You should have tried to explain. I know, I know, there didn't seem much point after what Stacey told you about her and Logan getting married. Land, child! You should have told me right away. I still can't believe it! If you'd told me I could have asked Logan myself."

Round and round the conversation went until Jill stood, ready to leave, feeling much much better for having talked with her friend.

"Better get moving, Jill," Aggie told her with a remorseful note in her voice, sorry to see Jill leave. She had really come to love the girl as her own. "Some of these roads are bad after dark. You leave me your address, and I'll get in touch with you as soon as I can."

Jill dried her tears. "You believe me, don't you, Aggie?"

" 'Course I believe you. Any woman would believe you. It's just men, Logan in particular, that don't believe." She grimaced. "I know it has something to do with being creative, him painting and all. I told you he sees what he sees and he hears what he hears. He wasn't always like this, but he's been hurt, and from the looks of things, he's gonna get hurt again. It's a sad fact of life, but it happens to be true."

Jill accepted a paper sack full of peanut butter cookies along with a thermos full of coffee. Tears blurring her vision, she embraced the older woman and was not surprised to see the faded blue eyes brim over.

"You drive carefully, you hear?"

Jill nodded as she climbed into the car. Doozey whined pitifully as he watched Jill pull out of the compound.

A week later, her honeymoon luggage stored in the basement, her honeymoon clothes sealed in plastic bags, Jill went back to the office. She was only working on a temporary basis, she reminded herself, until she could find another job. She knew she would see Deke and was prepared to handle it in the best way she could.

Jill felt her stomach heave with apprehension as she pressed the interoffice intercom and buzzed Deke's office. It had been easy to dodge him since her return, although tedious, for his working hours had become routine. It was only when Nancy had dropped off the claims marked for immediate attention that Jill admitted to herself that her game of hide-and-seek was only temporary.

"Mr. Atkins," she announced to the button-studded terminal on her desk, "there are some claims here that need your signature before they can be approved. Would you like me to bring them in now?"

"Jill? Jill, is that you?"

"Would you like me to bring in the claims now, Mr. Atkins?"

"Yes," Deke snapped, obviously stung by her cool behavior, "right away."

Deke's office was down the hall from Jill's desk and she walked toward it slowly, pacing each step as though she were walking to an early-morning execution.

Giving the door an announcing knock, Jill strode into the room, her demeanor hinting at a confidence she didn't really feel. Placing the papers on Deke's desk without a word, she turned to go but stopped short as he reached out and grabbed her by the wrist.

"Please, Jill," Deke whispered, his eyes begging, "sit down and let's talk."

"Deke, there's nothing to say."

Deke shook his head, pulling out a chair for Jill before he sat perched on the corner of his desk. "Perhaps you have nothing to say to me, Jill. I can understand that after everything that's happened. It's only that I was half out of my mind with worry. When you ran away, I thought that it would all work itself out if I didn't press you. I honestly tried to keep away from you."

"We were both wrong," Jill said quietly.

The statement somehow appeased Deke, for his face relaxed and he reached out to pull Jill to her feet. Embracing her, he looked down into her face.

"Knowing that, can't we try to start over again?"

Without a struggle, Jill let herself be led into a kiss, her mouth bruised as Deke pressed his lips against hers with a moan. She clung to him desperately, willing herself to respond. Instead, her mind conjured up Logan and the way her body had melted into his.

"You're crying," Deke observed, his fingers wiping the traitorous moisture from Jill's cheeks.

"We'll take things slowly," Deke promised. "There's no need to discuss our future together right now. We'll take it one day at a time . . . get to know each other again."

Deke held fast to his word. The weeks passed swiftly, each day bringing a new surprise as Deke stepped up his campaign to enchant Jill. A bouquet of flowers appeared at her door every day, sometimes accompanied by enormous boxes of candy, which remained stacked in Jill's refrigerator for the time when she felt compelled to binge. It was a time of wine, French restaurants and sojourns in Chinatown, a time to forget dreams of watching the sea by moonlight and tumbling passionately in the sand.

It was Saturday, and Jill awoke early, roused by a pounding at her door.

"Awaken, my lass!" Deke laughed as he leaned on her doorstep waiting to be invited in. "Your carriage awaits!"

Jill giggled. "Where are we going to-day?"

"You think I'm going to let the cat out of the bag?" Deke teased. "Get dressed and we'll see if you deserve to find out."

Deke drove for hours and Jill began to think that he was traveling in circles. When at last the car pulled to a stop, Jill considered herself completely lost.

Taking her by the hand, Deke led the way up a flight of enormous stone steps. The building that seemed to be his goal reminded Jill of the oversize library where she had spent many an hour during her childhood. The brick exterior was covered with trailing clumps of ivy, a square chunk of it kept trimmed beside the double glass doors at the front of the building to reveal a bronze plaque. Jill felt confused as she got close enough to read it. Barth Art Gallery.

From the interior of the building it was evident that the reputation of the gallery had once been very prestigious. Jill marveled that she had never heard of it before.

"How did you find this place, Deke?"

Deke pressed his finger to his lips, shaking his head as though sworn to secrecy.

It was the room reserved for the newest pieces into which Jill found herself being led. Most of the displays were sculptures, a few black and white etchings, and even some still photography. Jill was turning to Deke to demand an explanation when her eyes were caught by a solitary oil painting that had been given the honor of gracing one blank wall. She moved closer to it, her heart in her throat as she recognized Logan's style.

"I read about it in the papers this morning," Deke said from somewhere behind her. "It's that artist from Mill Valley. They had a whole write-up on him in the art section of the newspaper. He's had a big success in Paris, and he donated this painting to the curator of this gallery because the guy gave him one of his first breaks when he was starting out."

"I never mentioned Logan Matthews to you, Deke," Jill said, her insides aching as she felt all her longings for Logan renewed.

Deke flushed but didn't answer.

"You checked up on me?" Jill accused hotly.

"Of course I did!" Deke admitted. "How the hell was I supposed to know what was going on?"

Suddenly, it was all very clear, the truth drowning Jill in a whirlpool of resignation. Deke hadn't changed; he had only sat down and plotted out an intricate plan to wheedle his way back into her life.

"Take me home," Jill said calmly as she walked away from Logan's painting. "Take me home, Deke, and promise me that I'll never have to see you again."

"You'll change your mind, Jill," Deke warned as he dropped her off in front of her apartment. "You'll change your mind, and this time I won't be there."

Not looking back to answer, Jill walked up the stone path that led to her door and automatically took the mail from the box beside it before turning the key in the lock. Pressing her back against the solid support of the carved wood, she summarily sorted through the selection of bills and advertisements. Sticking out from the ordinary was an oversize pink envelope, Mrs. Beaumont's familiar scrawl taking up one whole side. Crossing to the couch, Jill sat down, propping her feet up on the coffee table. She managed a laugh as she pulled the letter out and smoothed it with the palm of her hand. It was written in pencil on the back of a sheet of crossword puzzles that Aggie had completed with great difficulty, evidenced by the smears of a soiled pencil eraser.

Dear Jill,

I've been meaning to write for some time, but as you know, it's time to close up the cottages for the winter and I've been busier than a spaniel with new pups. I got your letter and I am very happy that you're doing well and making a go of things. Every so often Doozey goes by the cottage and whines and yaps outside the door. I know he's looking for you. Logan is back in Boston. I'm sure, by now, you must have read about his success in Paris. It was in all the papers and one night he was on television. I was so proud I thought I would burst. Miss Phillips was married in New York. Logan gave her a painting for a wedding present. Logan didn't seem at all surprised or even hurt. He was real mad, though, that day you left. He mumbled something that sounded to me like "impatience of youth." He did ask me for your address before he went back to Boston.

Take good care of yourself, Jill. Think about me and Doozey out here walking the beach with the wind whipping about us. Both of us miss you. Have a nice Thanksgiving and a happy holiday season. Love from me and wet kisses from Doozey.

Aggie

Jill stared at the letter for a long time, rereading it until her tears made the words illegible. What had she done? Logan hadn't taken Stacey to Paris with him. Then why had he needed to book two seats on the airline? Could it have been for the dealer who had drawn up the contract at the showing that night? Jill sobbed, knowing that the details didn't matter. All she knew was that she loved Logan and she had allowed herself to walk away from him. Her life was crumbling around her, falling to pieces before her very eyes. It was as though her entire future flickered in the flame of a candle and she had been the one that had snuffed it out, pitching herself headfirst into darkness.

A week before Christmas, Jill made her decision. The arrangements had been so easy to make once she had made up her mind. She knew she could never return to the office as long as it held the certainty of daily confrontations with Deke. Her prospects appeared bright as she faced two interviews in the coming week. The packing had been the hardest. Her possessions had seemed so familiar in her apartment, and Jill wondered if they would ever fit another environment.

She had one last week to tie up all the loose ends. Her lunch on that day was a primitive one as she awaited the arrival of the moving van. Surrounded by all the packing crates, Jill was overcome with a mixture of emotions. She was positive that her entire life lay before her ready to be discovered. She felt sad as well, regretting that her past still haunted her.

When the movers called to report an emergency that would prevent them from coming today, Jill decided that she couldn't sit here in the apartment a moment longer. " 'Tis the season to be jolly," she hiccuped as she put on her coat. A trip into New York and a little Christmas shopping would perk up her mood. She was sure of it. Perhaps she could find a Christmas present for Aggie and have it sent. If there was a doubt that it would get to Mill Valley before Christmas, she would take the gift home with her and send it out with a belated card as soon as the holiday season was over.

Tramping and jostling her way through the holiday shoppers, Jill managed to lose herself in the spirit of the season. With gay abandon she purchased several brilliant bows and a sparkling gift wrap for the nonsensical little trinkets she had previously picked up for her friends. A few shining ornaments were bought with thoughtful consideration and wrapped in tissue paper. Each purchase was placed carefully in an oversized shopping bag with a brilliant Santa on the side.

How marvelous if the spirit of Christmas could be extended to take in the entire year! Goodwill and the cheer of the holiday season were contagious as Jill smiled and nodded to the harried shoppers.

Jill had one bad moment as she stood on the escalator in Macy's. She turned to admire the overhead decorations and the brilliant evergreen that looked so stunning from on high. She let her eyes fall to the milling shoppers and felt her heart lurch. Logan. Logan was standing in the sporting-goods department. It was Logan, she was sure of it. Jill stepped off the moving stairway and raced around to the other side, and actually walked down the steps in her eagerness to get to the bottom. Jostling and shouldering people out of her way, she ran past the tobacco shop and a display of wicker to the sporting-goods section. Her eyes searched frantically for some sign of Logan in his shearling jacket. He was nowhere in sight. She couldn't have been wrong. He had looked just like Logan. Surely, she hadn't been mistaken. She shook her head. She could never have mistaken someone else for him. There was only one Logan Matthews in the whole world, and she had just lost him for the second time.

Weary to the point of exhaustion, Jill made her way to a small snack bar. She waited patiently, her eyes searching the crowds as they flocked through the thriving department store. When she was finally ushered to a booth at the rear, she felt like crying. She had lost him again.

She gave her order of a Waldorf salad and black coffee to the waitress. Her shoulders slumped wearily. It was just the season for hope, she told herself. She wanted to see Logan, so somehow her mind conjured him up at just the right moment. If only Logan were with her it would be the perfect Christmas. She couldn't think of anything more blessed and peaceful than being in his arms. Holiday season or not, this dream was not meant to be.

Her mind was playing tricks on her again. Aggie had said Logan had asked for her address. Panic gripped her. If she moved from her tiny apartment, he would never find her. Visions of the packing cartons and the order form for the movers flashed before her. She couldn't move.

As she chewed her way through the crisp salad she first contemplated moving and then not moving. Logan. Aggie hadn't said when she gave Logan her address. Certainly, he had had plenty of time to get in touch with her if he had wanted to.

Boston was his home base. What could he possibly be doing here in New York at this time of year? Since he was a lawyer, it was logical to assume that he was on business for a client or even that the client resided here. If that was so, her mind questioned, what was he doing in the Macy's sporting-goods department wearing a shearling jacket?

She didn't have the answers. Jill pushed the salad plate away and picked up her coffee cup. She couldn't keep on torturing herself with maybes and what ifs or might have beens. She still had to find a suitable present for Aggie. She knew that if she really wanted more information concerning Logan, all she had to do was pick up the phone and call Aggie. Aggie would tell her whatever she knew.

Jill paid her check and walked back into the crowded mall, her thoughts concerned only with steering a straight course to the blanket department. She would get one of those new fashionable comforters so Aggie could toast herself in front of the fire, and, of course, a new super-deluxe bone for Doozey, or perhaps a new collar.

The salesgirl laughed mirthlessly when Jill asked if there was any way for the gift to arrive in time for Christmas. "What year?" she demanded.

Back in her apartment Jill looked around at the packing crates and felt sad. For the most part she had been happy in this apartment. What good was moving going to do? It seemed lately that all she did was run away.

Maybe what she should do was sit down and write Aggie a letter. No, it would be simpler to pick up the phone and call. On the other hand, she could pack a bag and drive to Rhode Island. She had no job now to worry about. Her rent was paid till the fifteenth of January. The tropical fish had long since found a new home with the elderly woman down the hall. There was nothing to keep her here. How she longed for Aggie's comforting presence and Doozey's jubilant affection. Why not? She would surprise both of them. Aggie would let her stay in her room with the twin beds.

Before she could change her mind, she wrapped Aggie's comforter and the dog collar for Doozey.

The first thing in the morning she would pack a small bag and leave. If she drove all day, she could make it by late evening.

Before she could change her mind, she called the movers and canceled her order to transport her furnishings and belongings to storage.

She felt better just knowing she was going to see Aggie and that the older woman would have some news of Logan. Just words. That was all she needed to help her get through the holiday season.

Nine

It was crisp and cold with more than a hint of snow in the air as Jill started out for Rhode Island. She felt exhilarated as her car sped along the open highway. She felt as though she were going home for Christmas. The feeling was so intoxicating that she started to sing under her breath. "Jingle bells, jingle bells," over and over.

Would Aggie have a Christmas tree? Was she the kind of person who baked and decorated the house for the holidays? If by some chance she didn't want to bother because she was alone, she, Jill, would do it for her. They would festoon the kitchens with evergreens and light big fires in the old stone fireplace. Aggie would wear her wrap comforter and Doozey would snooze in his new collar on the hearth. And Jill would putter around making both of them comfortable by making hot rum toddies.

She stopped once for a quick sandwich to take with her. She ate as she drove, not wanting to waste a minute.

It was shortly before dusk when the first snow started to fall. Jill cried out in excitement. There was nothing she loved more than a white Christmas. If only Logan were with her to share it! For now, thinking about him was almost as good as being with him.

By six o'clock the snow was falling heavily and the roads were becoming slippery. Jill slowed the car and made her way carefully. Another hour of cautious driving should get her into Mill Valley only an hour behind schedule. Lord, she was tired; her shoulders ached and her eyes were starting to burn with the close attention she was paying to the highway.

She skidded once and her heart leapt into her throat. To have come so far and have an accident now was unthinkable. She shifted the car into first and felt the wheels grab. That was better. She literally crawled as she made her way off the open highway onto one of the secondary roads that would lead her to Mill Valley and Logan Matthews' artists' colony.

The snow was coming down so fast she had to inch her way down the road. She peered out the open window for signs that she would remember. Her face and hair were soaked, but she could no longer see through the windshield.

The white sign with black lettering stood sentinel as Jill guided the car down the old road. Her tires made coarse tracks in the new-fallen snow. It was tricky going, but at least she knew she would meet no other vehicles on the road. The worst thing that could happen was that she would skid and careen into one of the ancient evergreens that lined the road.

Her first sight of the cottages and Logan's house sent a chill over her. She was home. This was where she wanted to be, where she needed to be — at least for the time being.

She was in the open compound now and driving carefully toward Logan's house. She parked in front, not sure exactly where the driveway was in the swirling snow. A faint yellow glow shone on one of the evergreens from Aggie's kitchen. Was she mistaken, or was that a bark? Could Doozey sense that she was back?

Jill cut the engine and pocketed the key. She struggled to get out of the compact car. How cramped and tired she was, yet she felt buoyed somehow. She was home; that must be it. She had just closed the front door and opened the door in the back to take out her bag when eighty pounds of dog leapt on her back, sending her sprawling onto the back seat.

Laughing and howling with happiness, Jill let the dog lick her face and her hair. "You aren't going to believe this, you dumb dog, but I've never been so happy to see anyone in my life. What have you been up to?"

Doozey cavorted in the snow, rolling and jumping like a puppy to show his delight with his new visitor. "Shh. I want to surprise Aggie. Come on, now; quiet is the name of the game." Jill could only assume the setter understood because he walked alongside her, licking her gloved hand.

Quietly, Jill opened the door and stared around the kitchen. Aggie was standing next to the stove, popping corn. She turned quickly, a look of alarm on her face, when she felt the cold draft from the open door. She pushed the popper to the back of the stove and grinned from ear to ear. "Well, I never," was all she said as she gathered Jill into a bone-crushing hug. "If you ain't just the best thing these old eyes could ever want to see. What are you doing here, child?"

"I came to spend Christmas with you. That's if it's okay with you."

"It's more than okay. But why would you want to lock yourself away here in the country with an old lady like me? Ain't nobody here but me and the dog."

"That's why I came. I was alone and knew

you would be too. I figured two loners should be together. Besides —" she giggled "— they said there was no way your present would get here in time so I brung it."

"You *brung* it, huh? Is that any way for a writer to talk?" Aggie laughed.

"It's okay for pretend writers who don't know any better. I'm hungry, Aggie."

"I expect you are. Take off those wet things and I'll fix you something. Here's a towel. Wrap your hair in it before you catch your death of cold and sit there by the fire."

"Are you going to have a Christmas tree, Aggie?"

"Wasn't planning on it, but I can see where I just changed my mind. There's boxes of decorations in the attic."

"Can we pop corn and string it on the tree?"

"You bet we can. I was just popping some now to put out for the birds tomorrow." Aggie gurgled with happiness. "Lord, child, you are a sight for sore eyes. Christmas always gets to me. Logan asks me each year to come to Boston to spend the holidays with him, but I don't belong there. I belong here, and here is where I stay. Me and Doozey make out fine. We get a little melancholy, but we manage."

Within minutes Aggie had a tray filled

and settled it on a small table near the fire. Jill had never smelled anything as good as the big bowl of thick vegetable soup. A wedge of French bread spread lavishly with butter made her hungry just looking at it. A generous helping of peach cobbler, along with a glass of creamy milk, completed her dinner. Jill devoured each morsel, savoring it. No one in the whole world could cook like Aggie.

"You look tuckered out. Why don't you sleep now and we'll talk tomorrow."

"Good idea, Aggie." Jill yawned. "But first you must tell me about Logan. Your letter said you gave him my address. Aggie, he never got in touch with me, not once." She hated the tremor in her voice and knew she was next to tears.

Aggie seemed to choose her words with care. "Honey, I told him everything you told me. I even called him a fool, a privilege he allows me from time to time. Logan, as I told you, he is not like most men. I don't ever remember Logan being in a position quite like this before. It's my opinion that he couldn't handle it, along with all of his successes in Paris. He knows he should have given you the chance to explain. But then you turned tail and ran. That was what made him think you lied to him. He was going to talk to you when he got back that day, but you were gone. Jill, in all fairness to Logan, you did lie to him. Logan never operates on a double standard. Seems to me both of you are at fault."

Jill nodded miserably.

"How is he, Aggie? A day didn't go by that I didn't think of him. Yesterday, I thought I saw him in Macy's. Does he have a shearling jacket, Aggie?"

"Yep, and a gorgeous thing it is. It probably was him you saw. He's in New York and has been for a week. I thought for sure he would have gotten in touch with you by now. Be patient, Jill."

"I love him," Jill said simply.

Aggie said nothing, but her eyes misted at the miserable look on Jill's face.

"You go along to bed now, and I'll clean up here. We have a lot of days ahead of us to talk."

"You're right, Aggie. I'll see you in the morning."

Long after the bedroom door closed, Aggie called for Doozey. Together they walked across the compound to the office. With the aid of a flashlight she picked up the phone and asked for the long-distance operator. Doozey barked his delight when he heard the tone of Aggie's voice.

By morning the deep tracks leading back and forth to the small office were obliterated by an additional ten inches of snow.

The following days were spent tramping through the woods looking for the perfect Christmas tree. Together Aggie and Jill chopped and sawed until the monstrous evergreen thundered to the ground. Heaving and struggling, they managed to slide the monster onto the sled they had brought along.

"Are we going to put it up in the kitchen next to the fireplace?" Jill asked, a note of hope in her voice.

"Of course. And we're going to string garlands all over the kitchen. I don't spend any time in the other part of the house and keep the heat down mostly to the kitchen, so that's the place for this beauty. Do you want to put it up tonight or wait till Christmas Eve?"

"Let's put it up but wait till Christmas Eve to decorate it. That's what we used to do when I was little."

"Then that's exactly what we'll do." Aggie laughed. "Remember, now, we have to bake a rum cake, a fruit cake and some cookies cut into Christmas shapes. I think I still have the old cookie cutters. I have a big turkey in the freezer, and I'm going to stuff it for our dinner. Tomorrow, we make the plum pudding and mince pie. A real old-fashioned Christmas. I'm real glad you came, Jill, and I'm just itching to see what's in that box you brought for me."

Jill laughed as she tugged at the heavy rope handles pulling the sled.

"I know you can't wait. No, you can't open it till Christmas Eve when we have our eggnog. Promise that you won't peek."

Aggie grinned. "I'm probably the oldest kid in these parts. If there's one thing I dearly love, it's to get a present. Always did love presents. Didn't matter what it was as long as it was wrapped up."

"Me too. I can't believe we really chopped down this tree," Jill said in amazement as she stared at the giant tree. "I think it's too big for the kitchen. We'll have to cut from the bottom."

With Aggie's New England practicality, they tied the branches together and were able to squeeze the tree through the back door. Huffing and puffing, together they managed to place it in the stand. The pine filled the kitchen with its scent, bringing the magic of Christmas indoors. Against the stolid background of fieldstone and brick, nature's greenery was set off to perfection.

"Oh, Aggie, it's beautiful," Jill whispered, the spirit of the holidays glowing in her eyes.

"Aye, it is that." Aggie beamed in approval. "Now for a nice hot cup of tea and we can begin making Logan's favorite gingerbread cookies."

At the sound of his name, Jill's eyes widened. "Logan?"

Aggie seemed to recover herself. "Er . . . yes. Logan's favorite. 'Course, they just happen to be a favorite of mine, too," she explained. "Now get the kettle on and I'll get the teacups."

After a day of baking and cleaning up, the wind seemed to have gone out of Aggie. "This is too much for you, Aggie. Maybe I never should have come."

"Don't say that, child. Christmas can be a lonely time for an old woman who has nothing to warm the holidays 'cept wood that she's chopped for herself and lots of old memories. Glad I am that you cared enough to come visit an old woman. As for being tired, you don't look so peppy yourself. I'm going to lie down and grab a few winks, and you should do the same."

Jill smiled, glad to be here with Aggie. "I will, I promise. But first you go. I'll finish out here, and then I want to write a few Christmas cards. Okay?"

"All right, but don't tire yourself out." Aggie's carpet slippers hardly made a sound on the linoleum floor as she made her way to her room.

As she had said, Jill finished washing the dishes and pans in the sink and put them away as she dried them. Every so often her eye was caught by the sight of the tree, and a little stab of melancholy made her brush a tear from her eye. Christmas, good cheer, peace on earth — would she ever find peace in a world without Logan?

Pushing away the thought of a lonely future, she snapped on the radio, playing it softly so as not to disturb Aggie. ". . . through the years we all will be together, if the fates allow . . ." The little stab of melancholy became an unexpected pang of sorrow, deep and profound. What she wanted most in the world was to share the holidays through the years with Logan. Sharing love, warmth — Stop it! she warned herself. Otherwise, you'll be a blubbering idiot and spoil Aggie's Christmas!

Sitting at the kitchen table, Jill finished her list of cards, signing each and every one of them "Love, Jill."

The teakettle whistled again, calling to her. Hurriedly, she jumped from her place at the table and went to the stove, nearly tripping on Doozey. "Doozey, love, you do have a way of getting underfoot."

Dunking her tea ball in and out of the tiny porcelain cup, Aggie's pride and joy, Jill stood near the window and gazed out at the winter wonderland. The snow was falling in big, fat flakes, but the sky was becoming brighter even for the late-afternoon hour. The storm would come to an end soon, and that special quiet would blanket the earth. Sighing deeply, she went back to the table to finish her cards. With the end of the storm, mail delivery would begin again as soon as the roads were cleared, which, Aggie assured her, would begin almost immediately. Here in New England, know-how and persistence were needed to keep the roads open in winter.

Sorting through the cards, Jill searched for her pen. A crunching noise caught her attention. "Doozey!" she scolded. "What have you done to my fifty-nine-cent ballpoint? Naughty dog!"

A search through her handbag was disappointing. No other pen. A look through the kitchen drawers turned up a pencil. Eager to finish her cards, Jill pushed through the kitchen door into Logan's study. Surely, there must be a pen on the desk.

With Doozey in close pursuit, she entered Logan's inner sanctum. The large, square room was full of the artist. Shelves of books lined two walls. A bay of windows looked out onto the drive and beyond, letting the wintry landscape into the house. Paintings, Logan's of course, filled the other wall. Here was the heart of the man — a slightly disordered desk that defied Aggie's attention, deep leather chairs and, most wonderful of all, a window seat nestled into the bay of glass. A carelessly tossed afghan supplied a splash of color against the dark shutters. Unable to resist temptation, Jill opened the shutters and was spellbound by the view. Hurrying back to the kitchen for her tea, she quickly reentered Logan's study and crawled up on the window seat, resting against the wall, feet tucked under the knitted shawl. The sky had become faintly gold, promising a beautiful sunset. She was determined to sit here and watch it, warmed by Aggie's tea and Doozey's presence beside her.

It was then that something caught her eye. Peeking from behind the sofa was the gilt corner edge of a picture frame. Curious that Logan should hide away a piece of his work, Jill was drawn to it.

The old sheeting that covered and protected it slipped away in her hands, and she gasped when she saw herself looking back from the canvas.

The sky outside brightened, illuminating the painting, bringing life to the colors Logan had placed there. Against the blue seashore, beside the familiar outcropping of rocks, pranced a white unicorn, and on his back was a slim, ivory-skinned girl whose long golden hair draped to her waist. And in the sky was the shimmering arc of a rainbow.

Jill sank to her knees. Logan had meant this painting to represent her. But when? The figure on the unicorn was vibrant with life. He must have painted it from memory; but how? Had she seemed so alive to him, so real? Had his fingers memorized her face? Had his hands chartered his memory with every curve and line of her body? Why?

Propping the painting against the sofa, Jill took her place on the window seat. Again and again her eyes were drawn to it, looking, searching for the inner woman that Logan had seen and rejected.

Ten

Christmas Eve was cold and bitterly crisp. The wind lifted the powdery snow and caused it to drift into patterns and shapes, disguising everyday objects beneath its whiteness.

Aggie was already busy in the kitchen when Jill crawled from beneath the covers, hurriedly dressing, eager to be in the warm kitchen. Delicious aromas surrounded her — spices, gingerbread, chocolate chip cookies, homemade breads and the beginnings of the turkey stuffing, tangy with sausages and chestnuts.

"Aggie? You must have been up for hours? Why didn't you waken me?"

"Have yourself a cup of coffee, Jill. I heard you prowling around most of the night and I know you didn't sleep well. It didn't seem right to get you up so early just because an old woman doesn't need as much sleep as some young person. Besides, you have a full day ahead of you, I promise you that," she added in a cryptic tone.

"And what's that supposed to mean?" Jill asked, pouring herself a mug of Aggie's fragrant brew.

"Oh, just that it's Christmas Eve and there's the tree to trim and food to prepare. . . ."

Looking around, Jill gasped. "Aggie, are you expecting the Army's Fourth Infantry? There's enough food here to feed them. I thought there was just going to be you and me."

"Well, there is . . . actually, sometimes the neighbors stop by and carolers . . ."

"Aggie —" Jill lifted a suspicious eyebrow "— carolers all the way out here from town when they know there isn't anybody here except you?"

"Well, child, some folks out this way are real neighborly, and, besides, maybe some people from church will stop out here on their way home. Didn't I tell you we go to Christmas services . . . ?"

Aggie continued to chat, her words and tone sounding nervous to Jill's ears. But soon she was lost in the preparations for tomorrow's dinner, peeling and slicing potatoes and mixing the ingredients for the Christmas pudding.

After stuffing pitted dates with walnuts and rolling them in sugar, Jill dusted her hands, surprised to see that it was nearly noontime. "Time to get the tree trimmings out of the attic."

"Now, wear your sweater," Aggie admonished. "Gets to be pretty cold up there. And be careful. I don't want you coming through the ceiling and breaking your leg."

All that afternoon, Aggie and Jill worked, humming along with carols played on the radio. Lemons and oranges, studded with cloves, were hung from the rafters, emitting their sweet smell. Yards and yards of popcorn draped the tree along with shiny balls and tinsel. Doozey, throwing himself into the holiday mood, sniffed the sweet, pungent air and begged for puffs of corn.

"This was an ornament from Logan's first Christmas tree," Aggie said proudly, holding up a fragile blown-glass clown whose colors had faded to soft pastels. "And here's another. I remember when me and my husband bought him his first tricycle. That child!" She laughed. "He'd whiz around this kitchen on that bike and my husband used to say he was hell on wheels. I was happy when spring came so he could ride it outside, I'll tell you."

The old memories clouded Aggie's face. "And see this one, Jill? It's a little gingerbread house. That was the year Logan was abed with the chicken pox. He sure was one sick little fella. Gave us some worry. He was six, that year."

As Jill tinkered with the ancient set of lights Aggie told her stories of Logan as a child. The memories softened the old woman's features, clouding her eyes. But her words were vivid, sharp with detail, and Jill imagined she could actually see little Logan pedaling his trike around the huge kitchen and praying for spring when he could take it outside and seek adventure. In those few short hours she learned more about the man she loved than any book could tell her.

When Aggie and Jill had finished putting away the last box, they stood back to admire their work. The kitchen had been transformed. Boughs of evergreen draped the exposed beams and the door lintels. Bright red ribbons added a gay note, and a myriad of candles stood waiting to be lighted. Everything was polished and gleaming, ready for the Night Before Christmas.

Aggie went about her last-minute chores humming "I'll Be Home for Christmas" and then switched to "I Wish You a Merry Christmas" when they went off to their bedrooms to dress for the church service.

Jill chose to wear a bright red woolen

dress that hugged her waist and fell in soft gathers over her hips. The little shirtfront with its button-down collar and short sleeves enhanced her diminutive figure. A simple addition of a gold chain and bracelet accompanied by tiny gold hoops in her ears were her only jewelry. Her shining, long blond hair was sleeked back and lifted onto the top of her head, its soft tendrils escaping and falling on her cheeks and the nape of her neck. The tall black boots gleamed in the lamplight.

A new beige cashmere coat, her only luxury in years, was belted at the waist. When she finally put on her bright red muffler and red gloves, she was ready.

"Coming, Aggie? I'm all set. What should I do with Doozey? He's not safe to leave alone in the kitchen. I'm convinced he can open the refrigerator door, and that would be the end of our Christmas dinner."

Aggie laughed. "Not to mention all the cookies and candies we baked. Better put him downstairs here in the bedroom where he can't do much damage."

Aggie looked lovely, her gray hair covered with a close-fitting fur hat and a black woolen coat. The galoshes on her feet did nothing to detract from her glowing face and sparkling eyes. On impulse, Jill snapped a tip from the Christmas tree and tied a red ribbon and two tiny Christmas balls to it. With the help of a safety pin, she placed the corsage on Aggie's collar.

"Now you're perfect, you really are, Aggie." Her voice was soft, on the edge of tears. "I want you to know that you've made this one of the happiest holidays I've ever known. I love you, Aggie."

"Pshaw, child, I knew that." Aggie wiped a tear from her eyes and hugged Jill tightly. "I feel as though you're my own child, and I only want the best for you. Sometimes I'm interfering and . . . and I just want you to know that whatever I do, it's because you mean the world to me. Come on now, or we'll be late."

The little yellow car hugged the road admirably, taking them the five miles to church. The black winter night sky was studded with stars, and in town colored Christmas lights dazzled the eye. The tall, steepled church was alive with light and humanity. People greeted one another and shook hands, wishing the best of the holidays. There was a peacefulness in the air, a reverence that shone from their eyes.

Inside was the scent of evergreens adorning the pulpit. Tiny candles glowed, and the choir stood at easy attention in their cranberry-colored robes. A nativity scene had been erected at the front of the church, and all eyes were turned to the empty manger that awaited the placement of the Christ-child figure at the stroke of twelve.

Aggie led the way into the pew, Jill right behind her. Although the church was crowded and every seat was needed, Aggie ignored Jill's proddings to push over instead of leaving room between herself and the last man on the long bench. The church filled rapidly, and several times someone came down the aisle expectantly waiting for Aggie to push in. Each time she refused.

The organ resounded from the rafters, filling the small interior of the church with music and voices. A hush fell over the congregation as the preacher took his place at the pulpit to recite the story of Christmas.

Jill's eyes touched on the people surrounding her. Husbands and wives, mothers and fathers . . . everyone seemed to have someone. Everyone but herself. Instinctively, she nestled closer to Aggie, appreciating the woman's presence and taking comfort from it. Everyone had someone and so did she. She had Aggie.

The minister instructed the congregation to all rise and open their hymnbooks to 139 — "Silent Night." Together, they lifted their voices in song, filling the small church with sound: "Silent night, holy night, all is calm, all is bright . . ."

A jostling at her elbow insisted that Jill move over. Remarkably, Aggie had slid over, making room, allowing Jill to admit the stranger beside her into the pew. Without looking up from her hymnbook, following the words to the carol's obscure second stanza, Jill continued to sing, lifting her voice along with the congregation's.

A bold hand took one side of her hymnbook, sharing it with her, and a deep, masculine voice joined hers in song. Jill turned, looking up, her knees nearly buckling under her. Logan.

His eyes smiled down at her.

Throughout the remainder of the service Jill's heart thumped madly in her chest. Logan! What was he doing here? Had he come expecting to find Aggie? Wasn't he supposed to be in Boston, New York, somewhere? Anywhere besides Mill Valley?

Toward the end of the service, when the choir's voices rang out the moving melody of "Ave Maria," Logan took her trembling hand in his. His fingers pressed an unspoken message into hers, and when Jill glanced at Aggie, the old woman had tears in her eyes and a smile on her face. She looked up at Jill, seeming to tell her that Logan's presence was Aggie's Christmas present to her.

Outside the church, Logan and Aggie renewed acquaintances, inviting people over to the house for eggnog and cookies. Logan introduced several of his friends to Jill, all the while draping his arm possessively around her shoulder.

During the trip back to the house Jill drove cautiously. Aggie was perched on the cramped back seat while Logan stretched his long legs beneath the dashboard. There were questions, so many questions, but somehow they would not come to her lips. She didn't want anything to spoil this night. Aggie kept the conversation alive by regaling Logan with stories of how she and Jill had found the perfect tree and decorated it, of all the cookies they had baked and of how Jill was fast becoming a first-rate cook. All the while Jill could feel Logan's eyes on her, watching her, smiling at her.

Before they could walk across the shoveled path to the back door, several cars had joined hers in the yard. People spilled forth, issuing glad tidings and good wishes. Inside, it was cozy and warm, and Aggie immediately lighted the many candles while Jill touched a taper to the firewood that had been laid. Logan greeted their guests and spoke of Christmases past while Jill and Aggie served eggnog and the various delicacies they had made with pride. Every so often when Jill turned, she would find Logan looking at her again, a strange light in his eyes.

Over the merry conversation in the expansive kitchen, voices were heard outside, ". . . We wish you a merry Christmas, we wish you . . ." Carolers! Someone exclaimed and they all rushed to the door to stand outside, shivering from the cold, to listen to the joyful sounds.

Jill pressed behind the crowd, and Aggie, in a flutter of motion, began bringing out more glasses and another tray of cookies for their songful visitors. An arm wrapped around Jill, warding off the cold. Logan. Always Logan.

As she gazed up at him she realized he was leading her back inside the house, through the kitchen and beyond the door, into his study.

Closing the door behind him, shutting out the intrusive sounds, he took her in his arms and pressed his face into her hair. "Umm, you smell so good. All soap and water. Kiss me, Jill." His finger lifted her chin, bringing her face up to his as he covered her mouth with his own in the sweetest, most tender kiss that seemed to last and last. And when he moved his lips from hers and looked into her upturned face, she could still feel the imprint of his mouth on hers.

"Merry Christmas, Jill." His voice was husky, deep with emotion. "I went to New Jersey, looking for you, you know. It wasn't till I heard from Aggie that I knew where you were. I would have been here sooner except for the snowstorm. . . ."

"Why?" she asked simply, her heart breaking with unanswered questions, questions which only Logan himself could answer.

Logan pulled her over to the window seat and sat down, holding her on his lap, nuzzling her neck. "Why did I leave you?" he asked.

Jill nodded, unable to speak, unable to break through the barrier of pain that had been with her since the last time she had seen him.

"Jill," he began softly, so softly, "I knew you were running away from something, someone. I was becoming too involved with you. That early morning on the beach I realized I loved you, with all my heart. I didn't want you to turn to me on the rebound. But when you answered my kisses, responded to my lovemaking, I lost myself in you. And heaven help me, that was what I had wanted and waited for all along. You, Jill. Only you. Whatever had come into my life before you was only a shadow, a cruel nightmare. I'd loved and lost once before, but never the way I knew I loved you."

"But you left me, Logan," she choked, whispering because she did not trust her voice.

"I told you then that you didn't know what love was all about. I was wrong. I even told myself I was wrong when I left you on the beach. I even went back looking for you, but you were gone. The next I saw you was here, at breakfast. And then . . . the . . ."

"Then Stacey Phillips found my discarded wedding gown. . . ."

"Yes. I cursed myself for being a fool. I believed you were looking for love on the rebound. I was hurt, Jill, so hurt. . . ."

"But I wasn't, Logan. You drove Deke out of my heart. You showed me what love was, something I'd never experienced before. . . ."

"And then I learned the story from Aggie. I thought it was too late. I went looking for you before I left for Paris. What I learned was that you were still seeing him. Then I learn you're here, with Aggie for

Christmas. . . . Jill," he breathed solemnly, "don't ever leave me again, not ever. I won't let you."

Jill snuggled closer on his lap, wrapping her arms around him, determined never to let him go. For a long moment they held each other, conveying their love. Logan's eyes fell on the painting he had done of Jill riding a unicorn. "I see you found it, the painting I've done of you. That's what you've done for me, sweetheart. You've made me a romantic, believing in the power of love. You've shown me the world of whimsy through your eyes and made me believe in unicorns and rainbows."

"You've made the world for me, Logan, in here." She placed his hand over her heart. "You've made the rainbows, the light after the storm."

Reaching around his neck, she pulled his face down to hers, lifting her mouth for his kiss. "Paint me rainbows, Logan," she breathed before his mouth touched hers and a riot of colors flared in her heart.

About the Author

This *New York Times* bestselling author has a passion for romance that stems from her passion for the other joys in her life — her family, animals and historic homes. She is usually found in New Jersey or South Carolina, where she is either tapping out stories on her computer or completing some kind of historical restoration. Legions of fans around the world thrill to the romantic stories Ms. Michaels creates in every one of her novels.